"It's not over between us, Deborah."

Jake's fingers moved sensuously against her throat. "Don't lie to yourself, and don't lie to me." His voice was hard. "I want you with a hunger that tears away at me twenty-four hours a day, a hunger I can't feed with anyone else."

Deborah's heart lurched violently. She felt raw hurt. She needed some defense against him and the feelings he could arouse in her so effortlessly. "I don't want to feel that way," she whispered in anguish.

"Do you think I do?" His eyes were burning with emotion.

He was talking about desire. He would never talk about love. She knew she was provoking an explosion, but she had to ask. "What about Leila? Isn't she still your lover?"

PATRICIA LAKE started reading romances when she worked as a library assistant in Birmingham, England. She didn't start writing, however, until she moved to the Yorkshire countryside. Her first book was completed in record time and when it was accepted for publication, she knew she'd found her niche in life.

Books by Patricia Lake

HARLEQUIN PRESENTS

These books may be available at your local bookseller.

Don't miss any of our special offers. Write to us at the following address for information on our newest releases.

Harlequin Reader Service
901 Fuhrmann Blvd., P.O. Box 1397, Buffalo, NY 14240
Canadian address: P.O. Box 2800, Postal Station A,
5170 Yonge St., Willowdale, Ont. M2N 6J3

PATRICIA LAKE

dark betrayal

Harlequin Books

TORONTO • NEW YORK • LONDON
AMSTERDAM • PARIS • SYDNEY • HAMBURG
STOCKHOLM • ATHENS • TOKYO • MILAN

Harlequin Presents first edition August 1986
ISBN 0-373-10907-5

Original hardcover edition published in 1986
by Mills & Boon Limited

CHAPTER ONE

'YOU will come?' Tess persisted, her voice faint and crackling, pleading long-distance.

Deborah stretched languidly, blinking, her eyes still not accustomed to the cool gloom inside the villa, after the brilliant sunshine outside. 'Tess . . . I don't know . . .' She felt uncertain, surprised by the invitation, by the long-distance telephone call. She hadn't heard from Tess in three years, and she and Oliver were not planning to return to England for at least another fortnight. Tess's big party was at the end of this week.

'Oh, Deborah, it's my twenty-first!' Tess wailed, annoyed at the prevarication. 'Everybody will be there. You *must* come—both of you, of course,' she added, hastily escalating her persuasion by including an invitation for Oliver.

Everybody? Deborah, still hesitating, felt a strange frisson of panic running down her spine. She wanted to ask if Jake would be there. Was that what Tess meant when she said everybody? But she didn't dare. It was too risky to even voice the question.

He'll be too busy, she told herself frantically while Tess waited impatiently for her answer on the other end of the line. Too busy to attend his sister's twenty-first birthday party? She was probably fooling only herself.

'I'll ask Oliver,' she said hurriedly, as the expensive seconds ticked by and she couldn't make a decision or even think of an excuse. 'And ring you back tomorrow—promise.'

'Deborah ... it's not because of what I said ... is it?' Without waiting for an answer, Tess continued. 'I didn't really mean it, you know—I was upset ...' Her voice faded, coming back stronger a second later. 'We can talk about it when we meet. I want to explain, to apologise.'

'It's all right, really, you don't have to explain ... I'll ring tomorrow.' Panic building, Deborah repeated herself almost desperately, and Tess was forced to accept the prevarication.

Seconds later, Deborah replaced the receiver and found that she was trembling violently. She pushed a hand through her fine blonde hair, all the relaxed languor of a morning's sunbathing gone in a flash, leaving her tense and haunted by memories she had been desperately trying to forget.

For the billionth time, Jake's dark serious face rose unbidden in her mind, bleak fury darkening his grey eyes, his mouth hard and cruel and sensual. That was how he had looked at her when they parted for the last time; when Deborah had run away, as far and as desperately as she could.

She shook her head, as though physically trying to dislodge the disturbing thoughts. She was still shivering, her body stiff with anguish. Three hellishly long years, she thought contemptuously, and still the thought of Jake sent her into a fever of despair.

Inside the villa, it was cool and dark, the terracotta tiles on the floors and the shuttered windows jealously guarding the lower temperature, closing out the heat beyond the walls. Deborah felt icy, suddenly frightened as she tried to blank out her thoughts. And she found herself almost running back out into the relentless sunlight, back to the deep glinting pool, and Oliver.

She watched him with concentration as she approached. Dear Oliver. He was the closest friend she had. He was her stepbrother, and although there was no blood tie, they were closer than brother and sister. Both only children of first marriages, they had come together happily, glad of the new, reassuring family life, until both parents had been killed when an articulated lorry skidded across the central reservation of the motorway, one dark winter afternoon. Deborah had been seventeen, suddenly alone, and had clung to Oliver in her grief, the bond between them growing stronger as time passed.

He was eight years older than her, a half-strong, half-weak vibrant man, whose perception and understanding of life was reflected in his vast paintings. He was a true artist, pouring all his emotion into his work, living on his nerves, his wits. Tall and thin, he had a quick jerky grace, his face tanned and so angelic, his eyes belying it all, wicked, worldly and intelligent. His tongue could fling acid and he veiled his feelings beneath an impenetrable flippant wit, that made him difficult to get to know. But he was always kind and protective towards Deborah. She never knew what he was really thinking, or what he really felt. But he was familiar, she knew she could turn to him. It was all they asked of each other, their love and affection always unspoken.

A few steps brought her to his side. He was stretched out on a lounger, idly reading a newspaper. They had spent the morning in the sun, swimming, drinking coffee and reading the English newspapers. This had been the pattern since she had arrived in Corfu, for a much-needed holiday. Neither of them had the inclination for anything too energetic.

Oliver looked up as she sat down, pushing his pale blond hair from his eyes, in a characteristic gesture.

'Who was it?' he demanded with a lazy smile.

Deborah looked at him, her eyes unfocused. 'Tess,' she revealed quietly, after a moment's silence. 'Tess Logan.'

Oliver's eyebrows lifted in surprise. He paused, then asked carefully. 'What did she want?'

It wasn't difficult to see that Deborah was upset, unsettled by the call. He knew how fragile she was, even after three years away from Jake Logan.

Deborah heard the carefully moderated concern in his voice, saw the worried look in his eyes, and made a concentrated effort to pull herself together.

Her lips moved in the semblance of a smile. 'It's her twenty-first birthday party at the end of this week. She's invited us both.' Her voice was almost steady, but she was cursing herself for being all kinds of a fool. What was the matter with her? Surely she wasn't going to crack up because Tess had invited her to a party?

Oliver narrowed his eyes against the sun. 'We don't have to go. We hadn't planned on going home for at least another two weeks.'

'I know.' Deborah was remembering the pleading note in Tess's voice.

At one time she and Tess had been good friends, close friends, almost like sisters. The last time they had met, Tess had been tearful and accusing. They had fought because of Jake, Tess fiercely loyal to her brother and, not knowing the truth of the situation, saying things that she obviously regretted now.

In a numb hurt way, Deborah had been able to understand Tess's anger. She still cared. Tess hadn't disguised how important the party, and Deborah's being there was to her.

Wouldn't it seem churlish and ungrateful not to give Tess the chance to deliver the apology she obviously thought so important?

'On the other hand,' Oliver remarked, still watching her carefully. 'It might just exorcise a few ghosts.'

Deborah didn't answer. She stood up, her eyes troubled. She didn't even want to think about it.

Poised on the tiled edge of the pool, she dived cleanly and surfaced, gasping. The water felt icy against her overheated skin. She glanced at Oliver as she trod water and shook back her wet hair. He was lying back, eyes closed, seemingly asleep. He had accepted her abrupt dismissal of the subject.

But she couldn't keep her thoughts at bay for ever, and that night she lay in the hushed darkness of her bedroom, and couldn't dam them back any longer.

She had been dozing, exhausted by the emotional strain of the day. She woke with a start, her heart pumping in her ears, Jake's name on her lips.

She looked round the room with wild eyes, straining to see in the darkness. She looked at the clock. She had only been in bed for an hour. It seemed like years.

Closing her eyes again, she sank back against the cool softness of the pillows. 'No,' she whispered, shaking her head. 'No.'

It was all starting up again. The nightmares, the pain, the terrible need. All triggered by Tess's innocent 'phone call.

Superficially she had been getting over it. She had been sleeping easier, even though she still thought of Jake twenty-four hours a day, even though he was still inextricably woven into every fibre of her being. She *had* been coping.

Sighing miserably, she climbed out of bed, knowing

that she wouldn't sleep, walked over to the windows and threw open the wooden shutters.

Outside, the night was clear, the moon high over the flat sea below, a faint scented breeze fanning her hot cheeks.

The dream was still too vivid in her mind, blocking out everything else. She could see nothing but Jake's face, the high tanned cheekbones, the hard powerful angle of his jaw, and his eyes, wild and dark and aggressive, gleaming like a wolf's in the night.

It seemed to her that his strength, his power reached out to her. Was he thinking of her now?

Her mind told her not to be so stupid, but her heart knew that somehow he was near, that incredible silent, explosive communication they had always shared, working again, whispering his threat across the miles.

She shuddered, her skin cold, her heart aching. It was over. *Over*. It was she who had lied, she who had run. And there was no going back.

Quietly opening her bedroom door, she crept silently into the small lounge and poured herself a small measure of scotch from the low table full of bottles.

She looked round the room, catching her own dark reflection in the long sliding windows. She was a tall slender figure wrapped in pale grey silk. Her hair was tousled, her green eyes too big in the delicate heart of her face. She stared anxiously at the tense reflection, hardly recognising herself, she felt so disorientated.

Was this how Jake had seen her? Had she looked like this when he lifted her into his powerful arms and carried her to his bed; on all those nights of fierce hungry passion, when he had taken everything and still demanded more?

Shivering violently in rejection of such memories, she curled up in the corner of one of the linen-covered couches, cradling the glass of scotch between trembling hands.

The room was filled with shadowy moonlight, the pale walls lined with Oliver's harsh paintings, their colours seeping away in the soft monochrome glare.

It was a beautiful room, very modern, very chic, all light and shade.

The villa belonged to Oliver now, payment for a series of portraits of an old titled family with little cash but plenty of property. It had been a good commission—and they were few and far between. Oliver had jumped at it with all of his customary lust for life, for experience and fame and fortune.

She sipped her scotch slowly, hating the taste but needing its calming effects.

Should she go to Tess's party? The question had been spinning round her brain all day, and she had been unable to come up with an answer.

Oliver had been no help at all. He had made it clear that as far as he was concerned, it was up to her to decide.

Over dinner, when she had tentatively raised the subject again, he had eyed her narrowly and said, 'Don't ask me, for God's sake, I'm not the one who's running away.'

And when she had protested, he had merely shrugged and added, 'Look, darling, just let me know when you've made up your mind, and in the meantime let's talk about something else, okay?'

And that had been that. Except that she couldn't make up her mind, however hard she tried.

It had taken all the courage she possessed to leave Jake three years ago. Since then she had been struggling to piece herself together, unable to become whole again because her heart would not stop aching.

Again and again her mind went back to their first meeting. She didn't know why, but today, she just couldn't get it out of her mind.

It had been too late for her the moment their eyes first met. If only she hadn't taken up her best friend Charlotte's offer of a stay in a tiny cottage in the Lake District. If only she hadn't felt so miserable and lonely. If only she'd gone to France and spent the summer with Oliver.

If only. Her life was filled with if onlys, and they didn't change a darned thing.

That summer had been so hot—the hottest on record, the radio had said. And Deborah was nineteen and wanting to be alone.

She had just finished her third year at Art College, and had a huge backlog of work to catch up on, owing to a bout of illness at the beginning of that year.

The cottage was tiny, beautiful and very old, nestling in isolation in the hills above Lake Windermere.

Deborah set up her easel on the stone-flagged kitchen floor and worked every day with the back door open and the lake shimmering away beneath her.

With Oliver away and most of her friends on holiday in various parts of the world, her loneliness enclosed her solidly but not unpleasantly.

She ached for love, for romance, for the closeness she had somehow missed since her father and stepmother had died. There were men in her life, of course. Fellow students, dear friends, like Robert, whom she had known from childhood. But none of them touched her heart, her involvement always half superficial, unsatisfactory.

She was shy, sensitive by nature, yet impulsive and deeply passionate, always ruled by her heart. Looking back, she could see how unprotected from the world she had been, how very vulnerable to the life and love she craved.

One blisteringly hot evening, a week or so after her arrival, she took a walk before preparing dinner, her back aching from the day's work.

The air was still and heavy, alive with summer insects and she walked eagerly, content to stare at the beauty around her.

She had discovered a wide deep stream not far from the cottage and strolled towards it.

The water looked cool and clear and inviting, and on impulse, first glancing round to check that there was nobody about, she stripped off her clothes and slithered down the grassy bank to the water.

It slid over her hot body like cold silk, intensely pleasurable and she swam, floated on her back, watching the sky tinged with pink at the edges as the sun began its slow descent.

It was so silent, so peaceful, only the birds, a faint rustling in the treetops, and the smell of summer all around her. Even now she could remember it all so vividly, every breath, every heartbeat. Every sense had been alive, exposed like cinematic film to the beauty around her, storing the images away never to be forgotten.

She stayed in the water for ages, cooling herself, until her stomach began to growl with hunger. Then she climbed out of the water, wringing out her hair, smoothing it back from her face into a gleaming golden cap.

As she raised her eyes, she had seen Jake for the very first time, crouching on the bank above her.

She froze, her heart stopping, her green eyes widening with shock. He was only a few feet away, but he was between her and the pile of hastily discarded clothes, and she felt the colour pouring into her face.

He didn't move, he didn't speak and she was frightened by his silence, receiving only the impression of his strength, his shoulders wide and powerful against the sky.

Her hands fell to her sides, dropping quickly. His face was in shadow until he moved slightly and their eyes met.

It was as though the impact was physical. He could have hit her and she wouldn't have been more shocked, more stunned. She stood perfectly still.

The man's eyes were grey, slightly narrowed as he stared at her. She could read no expression in them at all yet she could not look away.

As their glances locked for long inexplicably slow moments, Deborah felt a strange heat rising through her body, tensing the muscles of her stomach. She was no longer frightened or embarrassed, she felt only as though she was drowning in the grey depths of the stranger's eyes. Then, suddenly a huge magpie rose, flapping from the branches of a tree behind her. It's harsh cry filled the quiet air, making Deborah jump, bringing her back to some kind of reality.

She looked away, lowering her head, her face scarlet as she moved towards the pile of clothes.

'Excuse me . . .' Her voice shook a little, very cold.

He did not move. He was still and silent. She glanced at him from beneath her lashes, her breath catching in her throat. He was staring at her, his dark gaze moving over her naked body in slow masculine appraisal, lingering on the taut uptilted softness of her breasts, on the pale smoothness of her thighs.

Deborah felt as though she was suffocating, caught in some strange electric forcefield. To her own humiliation, she could feel herself responding mindlessly to the sensual awareness in the man's grey eyes. Her breasts were aching heavily, the muscles of her body clenching. His cool gaze returned to her flushed face. Swallowing painfully, she stammered. 'Go away, I want to get dressed.'

The spell was broken. She could feel cold water dripping from her hair down her spine.

The man moved in one lithe movement, rising to his feet. He was tall, well over six feet, his body strong and powerfully muscled.

In silence he turned away, moving a few feet to lean against a wide tree trunk, his back to her.

Deborah stared at him for a few seconds, a sense of unreality gripping her. She heard the metallic click of a lighter, the faint aroma of Turkish tobacco. He was smoking a cigarette.

She shuddered violently and began pulling on her clothes as quickly as she could. They stuck to her wet body uncomfortably and her hands were shaking.

It must be late, she decided, as she pulled tight the belt of her jeans. The sky was darkening, striped with yellow and purple and deep dusty pink. The trees were darker, powerful silhouettes against the fire of the sky.

She pushed back her hair, and cast another furtive glance at the man who stood only feet away from her. Her heart beat faster as she began to move, hoping to get away before he noticed. But in her agitation, she didn't move silently. Twigs cracked noisily beneath her sandals and as she looked over her shoulder, she saw that he had heard her frantic escape. Her foot caught in a slender tree root poking up from the soil and she lost her balance, falling towards the ground.

It all happened in a second but again she had that feeling that everything was moving in slow motion. The man moved with swift panther-like grace, covering the distance between them so quickly. He caught her before she hit the ground, pulling her up against his hard body, steadying her.

She felt the strong grip of his hands against her shoulders, burning through the thin material of her T-shirt, as he set her back on her feet.

She looked up into his dark face, her head falling back, and the breath caught sharply in her throat.

Out of the shadow, she could see him clearly now. She guessed he was in his mid to late thirties, much older than the men she was used to.

He had a hard-boned serious face, all planes and angles, the cheekbones high beneath smooth tanned skin, the jaw harsh and uncompromising. His hair was almost black, brushed back from his face, touching the collar of his shirt at the back. His mouth was strong and beautifully moulded, but it was his eyes that held her attention, that held her wide gaze with no effort at all. A dark narrowed grey, beneath black sweeping brows, they mirrored his experience, his wisdom and something else—a shadowed unsmiling expression that Deborah could not understand.

She dragged her own eyes away with a great effort of will, her heart pounding.

'Thank you.' The murmured gratitude came out breathlessly.

In silence the man released his grip on her shoulders, his hands falling to his sides, and Deborah felt strangely bereft.

She turned away, unable to think coherently, her mind chaotic. From that moment on, it was always that way. His touch, his mere presence had been enough to drive any sane thoughts from her head. She had known from that very first moment that her life would never be the same again. One glance at him had warned her that he was a man who lived by his own rules, a man who faced the world alone and forced it to give him what he wanted. He was sure of himself as only the wise and the strong can be. He was everything she had ever dreamed about in a man.

That first summer evening, he had walked her back to the cottage, despite her trembling protests. They had not talked much. He had seemed pre-occupied with his own thoughts, brooding, silent. And Deborah had kept her head down, shy and flustered by his attention, ridiculously tongue-tied for the first time in her life.

He had introduced himself as Jake Logan. Even his name was hard and strong and uncompromising, and of course, she recognised it immediately. He was a brilliant, much acclaimed playwright, lionised in both England and the United States. His plays were complex and sensitive, enjoying long, fantastically successful runs.

Incredibly, his identity hadn't surprised her. There was something about him that told of power and success, something cool and hard and indefinable.

He had taken her out to dinner the following evening. Deborah was already wildly and irrevocably in love with him. She was hardly able to eat a thing at the discreetly expensive hotel restaurant in Windermere. He had made her laugh that evening. His easy charismatic charm had knocked her off her feet, and somehow he had elicited her life story, storing away every careful detail almost before she realised she had opened her mouth.

Back at his huge old house in the early hours of the next morning, she had prowled the rooms with delight, staring out of the ceiling-high panoramic windows at the clouded fells, bright beneath the silver moonlight, at the dark mysterious lake beneath them. And she had denied herself by thinking that she wouldn't sleep with him.

He was almost a stranger, and how could she be so fiercely in love with a stranger? How could she have looked into those dark grey eyes and lost herself so completely?

Unknown to her, Jake watched the secret smile that touched her vulnerable mouth. She let her hands drift over a bronze statue that stood in front of the window.

Wasn't this what she had longed for, ached for? A love like this? The deeply-passionate, unconventional, impulsive side of her was straining towards the night's inevitable conclusion. And when she turned round to find Jake staring at her, any doubts had melted away like snow in tropical sunshine.

He hadn't pushed her or forced her. He had only reached for her, his powerful hands strangely gentle, his eyes very dark, hypnotising her. The touch of his mouth had made her burn with emotion and a desire so strong and all-encompassing that it overwhelmed her.

As he touched her, caressed her, kissed her, unable to disguise his hunger for her, she responded mindlessly, aware of her power over him, aware that he was teaching her about love, about herself. He was teaching her things she had never even dreamed of.

And when he finally raised his dark head, and held

her away as he regained his sanity, her eyes had mirrored her surprised confusion. Her smile was that of a temptress when he told her he was taking her home—immediately, before he couldn't help himself. In reply she had pulled down his head, using her innocent mouth and her tentative fingers until he could not resist her.

Jake had given her a fulfillment she hadn't believed herself capable of. She remembered the smooth hard warmth of his body, the strength of his taut muscles, the hungry expertise of his mouth.

Oh yes, Jake had taught her everything about love, about herself, but he had also taught her about need and jealousy . . .

'Can't you sleep either? This bloody heat . . .' Oliver's voice cut into her deep reverie, making her jump.

She hadn't even noticed him entering the lounge. He switched on one of the lamps, cursing under his breath as his toe connected with the leg of the table.

'Why the hell are you sitting in the dark?' He sounded irritated. He hated it when he couldn't sleep. He hated anything that interfered with the rhythm he had created for his life.

Deborah looked up at him, still far away, blinking against the sudden glare of light.

'I'm thinking.' Her voice sounded small. The memories of Jake still hurt her, more than she cared to admit even to herself.

'Oh.' Oliver's one word held a wealth of meaning. He walked over and poured himself a large measure of scotch, then moved across to the window, where he stood staring out into the darkness.

Deborah watched him, absently staring at his lean brown body above the cotton shorts he wore.

'This must be the hottest summer I can remember,' Oliver remarked as he swallowed back his scotch.

'Yes, I suppose so,' Deborah answered vaguely, but she was thinking, no, the hottest summer was the one I spent with Jake. It said so on the radio.

Oliver turned, reaching for a cigarette. 'It's Logan, isn't it?' he said, touching a flaring match to the tobacco. 'Why, in God's name can't you just forget him? How long are you going to torture yourself?'

Deborah shrugged, ignoring his anger. There had never been any love lost between Jake and her stepbrother. Oliver had seen that violent possessive side of Jake, he had been on the receiving end of it. Oliver hated violence in any shape or form, and Jake's dark savagery had scared the hell out of him. He had freely admitted that.

He was impatient with Deborah for not putting the whole thing behind her. He watched the tell-tale signs now and his face softened as he said casually, 'Do you want to talk about it?'

She smiled knowing he was making an effort to curb his irritation. 'Thanks, but I don't think so.'

'As you wish.' He seemed unconcerned, drawing deeply on his cigarette and turning back towards the window.

Deborah looked at him, his shoulders hunched against the long bleached linen curtains. They knew each other very well and she suddenly realised that it wasn't just the heat that was keeping him awake.

'What's the matter?' she asked quietly, glad to be able to think about him, to shift her mind from herself.

Oliver was silent for a moment, then he turned to look at her, smiling wryly. 'Clever. For a girl so wrapped up in her own problems, you're surprisingly perceptive tonight.'

Deborah stood up, took his glass, and poured them both another Scotch, passing his, then curling up on the sofa with her own.

'So, tell me,' she prompted lightly. Oliver sighed, his face hard. 'Beatrice rang this afternoon, while you were in town.'

Deborah bit her lip. No wonder he had been so sharp with her all evening. 'And?'

'And she asked if she could fly out for a few days. Said she needed a break.' Oliver swallowed down his scotch in one long mouthful, his eyes lowered.

'Does she know I'm here? What did you tell her?' Deborah stared, surprised. He had not mentioned it over dinner, or any time during the evening.

'I told her that she couldn't come, that I was busy— too busy to fool around with her.'

'Oh, Oliver.' She was suddenly sad, knowing what it must have cost him to turn Beatrice down.

'Oh, Oliver, what?' He mimicked her voice, not unkindly, but with a wry self-deprecating mockery. 'There was nothing else I could do.' His shoulders lifted. 'God, I could even hear David talking on another 'phone.'

'Then, why was she——'

Oliver didn't let her finish, his eyes shadowed as he said bitterly. 'Who knows? Another rough patch, maybe. She was probably trying to hurt him, or was she just trying to use me? Either way, I can't take any more of it. I can't even fool myself that it's going somewhere.'

Deborah sighed, her heart aching. Beatrice Maitland was a beautiful woman, a married woman. Oliver was deeply involved with her, fighting a love that was far too strong, in his battle to free himself. Beatrice was a fashion model who worked for Deborah's boss Cole Sullivan, modelling the clothes Deborah designed. Oliver had been introduced to Beatrice at a party thrown by Cole at his London flat, a year or so ago.

Deborah had dragged Oliver along because he had been moping round the house, utterly depressed. The painting he had been working on refused to come together. He couldn't paint. It was incredible he had ever thought he could. He might just as well give up his career and get a job as an insurance salesman. He went on and on as she dressed for the party. She had ignored him. She had heard it all before.

Beatrice Maitland had dominated the room, and, she had taken one look at Oliver's blond good looks and moved in.

After that they had rarely been seen apart. Beatrice had left her husband a month before she met Oliver, and she was more than ready for Oliver's eager attention.

And although their relationship had been stormy and passionate, Deborah had only realised Oliver's desperate involvement when Beatrice returned to her husband David, six months later.

Since then, it had been an on-off thing. Oliver had tried to keep away from Beatrice, and Deborah was fully aware of what that had cost him. Beatrice's marriage was by no means perfect and she kept Oliver on a string, knowing that he loved her too much to resist.

It was an impossible situation and Deborah had come very near to hating the beautiful model.

Oliver had changed with this love. He drank heavily now, hating himself for his weakness, though the walls of his flat were lined with photographs and drawings of Beatrice. His work was suffering, too. He was subject to bouts of deep depression, all hidden carefully beneath that sharp tongue and flippant mask.

Nobody else guessed except Deborah and that was only because they shared the same house and he could not hide behind his mask twenty-four hours a day.

Sometimes she felt responsible. If she hadn't dragged him to that party . . .

And sometimes she tried to imagine how it would all end. David Maitland was rich and successful and Deborah secretly wondered if Beatrice would ever leave him. It seemed she valued material wealth above all else.

She looked at her stepbrother now, and knew exactly how he felt.

'Perhaps . . .' she began, unable to bear the weariness she saw in his face, wanting to reassure him in some way.

'I'm going back to bed,' he cut in, rejecting her sympathy before it was uttered. 'I want to go to Paleokastritsa tomorrow, to take some more photos. Do you fancy coming with me?'

Deborah nodded, pushing back her pale hair. 'Yes. Early?'

'As soon as it's light, that's the best time.'

He walked towards the door, stopping to look back at her. 'Have you decided about Tess's party yet?'

'No.' Deborah's voice held all her uncertainty.

'Well, I think we should go.'

It was the first positive thing he'd said about it, and Deborah's head jerked up. 'Why?' she asked baldly.

'You know very well.' He half-smiled.

'But if——'

'If Logan is there, so what? It's more than likely

that he will be. You can cope, and anyway, I'll be with you.'

'I'll decide tomorrow.' She had been thinking of Jake, remembering so painfully she couldn't make the decision until her mind was clear of those memories.

'Don't be a coward, Deborah,' Oliver said wickedly, watching her flushed cheeks and lowered eyes.

'Like you?' she retorted, stung.

'Yes, like me,' he agreed, without malice, then laughed. 'I'll see you in the morning. Don't forget, dawn.'

She didn't answer, listening to the slamming of his bedroom door, and then to the silence broken only by the whirring of the crickets in the garden outside.

It looked as though she had backed herself into a corner. Of course she would have to go to the party. She couldn't hurt Tess. And there was no guarantee that Jake would be there.

And if he is? a tiny voice in her head argued. If he is, will you be able to face seeing him again? She couldn't answer that. She couldn't even begin to imagine how she would react if she met him face to face. She had spent the past three years trying to avoid such a meeting.

Soon after they had parted she had met Cole, through Oliver's introduction and had jumped at the offer of working in his Los Angeles headquarters for nine months.

She had nearly bitten his hand off, terrified of running into Jake in London. And those months in America had helped, the furious, totally alien pace of downtown Los Angeles forcing her to concentrate, to forget her own pain for hours at a time.

By the time she returned to England the fear had

lessened. And apart from the three tragic months of her marriage, she had spent the last couple of years between Los Angeles and London. In all that time she had seen Jake only twice. The first time, although only at a distance, had hurt her so much that she had stood paralysed, unable to move a muscle. She could remember it so clearly. She had been shopping on Bond Street, a last minute birthday present for Cole, gold cufflinks specially engraved. She had slipped out of the studio for an hour, hoping that nobody would notice her absence, and had been emerging from the jewellers when she saw Jake on the other side of the road. He was talking to another man who she barely registered. Her eyes were fixed on Jake with a shaming intensity.

He was smiling, that cool charming smile that had always turned her knees to water, his eyes narrowed, faintly cynical.

She watched him push an impatient hand through the darkness of his hair, a painfully familiar gesture that squeezed her heart with agony. Every easy, graceful movement he made had registered like physical blows, her eyes hungry on the powerful masculinity of his body. Then he was gone, sliding inside the long black chauffeur-driven car, disappearing in seconds, so that she wasn't sure whether or not it had all been a wishful dream. He had not seen her. Ridiculously that had hurt, although she had been unable to think of one good reason why it should.

That tiny incident kept her alive, and depressed her terribly for months afterwards. It wasn't the same as seeing him in the newspapers, reading about the success of his plays, the latest beautiful woman he was being seen around with, as she always did with an eagerness that made her hate herself. It wasn't the same at all. It changed her, hardening the protective shell she had built around herself.

As she thought of it now, she wondered whether she had the strength to face him again. She stood up, slowly walking to the windows, staring down at the dark mysterious Mediterranean. And yet, she thought fatalistically, what choice did she have if she ever wanted to get over him.

'Oh God, Jake,' she whispered aloud, pressing her face to the smooth, cool glass. 'When will I ever be free of you?'

CHAPTER TWO

OLIVER'S villa was situated in the hills above Benitses, on the east coast of Corfu, so it was a fairly long drive to Paleokastritsa.

Deborah woke before dawn after a restless, almost sleepless night. She pulled herself tiredly out of bed aware that the sun would soon be up. Her brief snatches of sleep had been haunted by dreams of Jake, and in the darkness before dawn it was hopelessly depressing to realise that the thin shell of emotional strength she had been building up over the past three years was still fragile enough to come crashing around her ears at Tess's telephone call.

Angry at her own inability to control her feelings, she showered and quickly dressed in jeans cut off at the knees, and a sleeveless T-shirt.

Looking at herself in the mirror as she brushed and plaited her long fair hair, she grimaced at the dark circles beneath her eyes. She looked a mess, she felt a mess, and she didn't know what to do about it.

She found Oliver making coffee in the kitchen. He greeted her cheerfully but she had the feeling that he hadn't slept any better than she had.

Outside, through the open doors, the sun was beginning to lighten the horizon, the gnarled old olive trees catching the first rays of light.

Deborah couldn't touch any food, but watched Oliver eating an orange with his coffee, her thoughts miles away.

They left the villa within half an hour, the jeep

Oliver had hired for their stay, bouncing easily over
the rough track towards the narrow road. Deborah
pushed her sunglasses on to her head and gazed at the
wild flowers that carpeted the ground beneath olive
and cyprus and poplar. The air was as new as the day,
fresh and still cool. Corfu was such a beautiful island,
she thought lazily, so barren and harsh despite the
greenery.

Before they reached the main road, they were forced
to slow down behind an old man and woman with a
donkey. The man sat astride the slow donkey, the
woman, small and bent and dressed in black from head
to toe was walking ahead. They waved as the track
finally became wide enough for the jeep to pass.

'Equality,' Oliver laughed, raising his hand.

Deborah smiled. 'That's one way of looking at it, I
suppose,' she said, unable to shake off the weary
bleakness of her mood.

They drove along the steep winding road into
Kerkira, the capital, slowing to match the pace of the
heavier traffic. Deborah stared out at the crumbling
forts that overlooked the sea entrance to the town and
tried to shake off her strange mood.

'I want to buy some film, so let's have coffee here.'
Impatient with the queues of traffic, Oliver pulled into
a parking space near the harbour and jumped out of
the jeep.

They walked through the narrow venetian streets,
the high balconies above them strung with washing
and lined with gaudy flowering plants. It was still very
early but the town was bustling with activity. Deborah
was feeling lazy, so while Oliver purchased his film,
she sat beneath the tall archways of an outdoor café,
sipping thick dark coffee and watching the world go
by, happy to be alone.

They reached Paleokastritsa before noon, approaching above the clover-leaf Bay of Alipa, past huge private villas, most lost to view behind banks of flowers, bushes and trees.

It was busy, crowded with well-oiled noisy tourists, and the sun was relentlessly hot. They ate salad rich with Feta cheese and bitter olives, at a *taverna* near the water's edge. Lobster was the local speciality, kept alive till ordered. It seemed horribly cruel to Deborah and she wouldn't have dreamed of ordering it. The sheer beauty of her surroundings brought back her appetite and she ate her salad with relish.

Oliver was bright and seemingly cheerful. Neither mentioned the night before, neither mentioned Tess's party.

The white monastery on the clifftops was as Deborah remembered, with its white-washed towers and heavy metal bells. Leaving Oliver to his work, she walked alone into the cool dark church. It was believed that the monastery had been founded in the thirteenth century, though the present buildings were nineteenth and eighteenth century.

She wandered around gazing up at the painted ceiling and silver chandeliers, at the icons in their carved gilt frames. She glanced at a forgotten guide book that suggested from the work of Berard that Paleokastritsa was the site of the Phaeacian capitol in Homer's Odyssey. That sort of detail would have fascinated Jake . . .

The booklet dropped from her hands unnoticed, and she closed her eyes. She hadn't done that for months. It had been a difficult habit to stop, seeing things through his eyes, knowing what he would appreciate, needing to share her experience with him.

Disturbed, she walked out into the blinding

sunshine of the courtyard, walking beneath cane trellises, the scent of flowers and herbs filling her nostrils.

He was always there in the back of her mind, brought into her thoughts at any opportunity. She caught sight of Oliver, waving as he disappeared behind a low terracotta-roofed building.

She lifted her hand automatically, her mouth moving in the shape of a smile. Below lay the calm blue sea, broken by huge red rocks that rose like towers from the water to the sky, the horizon barely discernible between.

This view always stilled her and she longed for someone to share it with. Someone? Who was she kidding? She wanted Jake. She had never stopped wanting him and she couldn't deny that any longer. Despite that dark violent side to his nature, she still cared, still needed him.

Her thoughts drifted back to that summer in Windermere. A couple of weeks was all they'd had, but it seemed a lifetime.

She had left her work in the tiny cottage unfinished. She didn't care. It meant nothing. All that mattered was being with Jake, and every second had been unbearably precious. They had spent their days walking and sailing, lying at the lakeside in the sun, talking and making love. When she looked back on it now, the sheer silent intensity of her feelings then frightened her. She had been so young, so fierce and Jake was totally unlike any man she had ever met, his personality strong and complex and self-assured. She realised later that he had hardly ever talked about himself, persuading her to talk instead, as though he needed to know every little thing about her.

And at night she would lie in his bed, held tightly in

the powerful, possessive circle of his arms, hardly daring to sleep in case she woke and found it only a dream.

It satisfied her to know that he had come from London to write, yet, since their meeting, he had not written a word of the play so eagerly awaited by the West End.

'God knows, I can't think of anything but you,' he had murmured into the loose golden silk of her hair. 'You're so beautiful, so soft.'

And Deborah, lonely no more, with everything she had ever longed for, had smiled and touched her mouth to his.

Those brief days had been idyllic, too wonderful to last. She knew now, with unusual cynicism, that nothing of any great value lasted.

As the days passed she had gradually found out more about him, though he hadn't told her easily. His childhood, his whole life had been unconventional, marred by tragedy. His father had walked out on his mother, a week before Jake was born. His father had been a famous concert pianist, Jake the product of a brief passionate affair. The concert pianist died two years later never knowing his illegitimate son. Jake had been brought up in the house of his grandfather, who he spoke of with deep love and affection. Sander Logan had been the only father Jake had known, a strong friend in his formative years.

Years later, his mother had married disastrously, and Tess had been born. That marriage had ended in divorce within two years, his mother dying quickly and unexpectedly when Tess was twelve.

It was a powerful story, though Jake seemed untouched by it all, uncaring. He had travelled widely with his mother when he was a child, and alone, on leaving school. He was a man of experience, of perception. He had a sharp sense of humour, he could laugh at himself and he could laugh at the world, and nothing in those cool grey eyes ever revealed the turbulence of his youth. It was only much later, back in London that Deborah had seen that dark possessive streak in him, perhaps the effect of his upbringing, certainly the core of his brilliance as a playwright.

'Hey, look who I've found!'

She opened her eyes, blinking against the sun, and forced her lips to smile. Oliver was striding towards her, followed by Cole and his ex-wife Janetta.

It was a huge surprise. Cole was the last person she had expected to see here in Paleokastritsa.

'What on earth are you doing here?' she demanded, laughing, her smile for real now as she moved towards him.

Cole kissed her cheek, his blue eyes narrowed against the sun, their depths lazily amused. 'You've caught the sun. A tan suits you.'

'Which doesn't tell me anything, does it?' Used to his careless compliments, his affection, Deborah turned to the beautiful woman at his side. 'How are you, Janetta? It's been ages.'

'Too long, darling. You look wonderful.' Janetta squeezed her hand.

She was the same age as Cole, late thirties, but she looked much younger, her skin pale and perfect, flawlessly made-up beneath a wide straw hat. Her hair was deep auburn, curling with effortless chic around the sculptured triangle of her face.

Deborah looked down at her own scruffy, cut-off jeans, then at Janetta's pale linen sundress, and grimaced inwardly. Despite the older woman's

kindness and genuine friendliness, she always felt
gauche by comparison, childish.

'I doubt it, but thanks anyway,' she smiled.

Cole slid his arm around Janetta's shoulders, his
eyes on Deborah. 'Such a modest, unassuming child,
isn't she?'

Deborah laughed, and Janetta turned to Cole, her
eyes warm. 'Don't tease, darling. Deborah may never
forgive you.' There was a slight sharpness in her voice
that Deborah couldn't identify.

'Oh, I'm well used to it,' she said airily. 'He's a hard
taskmaster—very difficult.'

'You don't have to tell me.' Janetta's remark was
heartfelt, though not very serious.

She and Cole had been childhood sweethearts,
married at eighteen, divorced two years later. 'We
were too close—we couldn't live together for more
than five minutes at one time. We drove each other
crazy,' Cole told Deborah, the first time she was
introduced to Janetta.

They were still very close though the best of
friends. 'No regrets,' were Cole's own words, but
sometimes when Deborah looked at Janetta, she
wondered if the older woman felt the same way. There
was still something there in her eyes when she looked
at her former husband, something undefinable but
definitely at odds with Cole's breezy 'No regrets'. But
it was none of Deborah's business and she didn't dare
to pry. In some ways Cole was a very private man. She
had no idea how he really felt, she only heard his
complaints about the vast amounts of alimony he had
to pay to Janetta and his assertions that the beautiful
women he was seen around with were all 'strictly
casual—no strings attached.'

'You must have dinner with us tonight at our hotel.'

Cole looked from Deborah to Oliver, persuading them with his smile. 'The food's pretty good.' Oliver's eyes told Deborah that he had nothing planned, so she accepted for both of them. 'That would be lovely. We didn't have anything arranged for tonight.'

She wanted to shower and change, so they arranged to meet at the hotel after nine. The drive back to Benitses was pleasant. The sun was losing its heat, the sky paling from relentless azure to a delicate cornflower blue. Deborah leant back and allowed the cool breeze to whip her hair around her face. She was angry with her own lethargy, the grey depression that was lurking just beneath the surface. Oliver chatted and she responded automatically, a trick she had learned very well over the past three years.

They reached the villa in plenty of time, despite the traffic in Kerkira. The maid was just leaving as they walked through the wooden front door. Maria, a very quiet girl with a sweet smile and hardly any English, came from the village every other day to clean.

She smiled at Deborah and Oliver. 'Laundry,' she said haltingly, the word broken and alien.

They both smiled. 'Thank you,' Oliver said carefully. The girl nodded, her face shy, and disappeared.

'Drink?' Oliver flung down his camera and walked over to the stock of bottles.

'Gin and tonic, please,' Deborah kicked off her sandals. 'I think you've made another conquest there.'

'What?' Oliver turned from his task, his eyes innocent.

'Maria.' She flung open the long wooden shutters to admit the cooler afternoon air.

Oliver snorted as he passed her a glass frosted with ice.

'Oh, so you've noticed,' she teased.

The jangle of the telephone broke between them. Oliver stiffened imperceptibly, pretending to be busy with something else, so that Deborah reached for the receiver. 'Hello?'

It was Beatrice. 'Deborah darling, is Oliver about?' Her voice was warm and husky, very attractive.

'Beatrice—how are you?' She gave the clue easily to Oliver, who shook his head, his face whitening. 'I'm not here,' he mouthed silently.

Deborah nodded, only half listening to Beatrice, her sympathy and attention with her stepbrother. 'I'm afraid Oliver isn't here at the moment. He's driven down to Benitses to get some film developed.' She found it difficult to tell the bare-faced lie, adding to lend weight to it, 'We went to Paleokastritsa and Oliver took hundreds of photos.'

Amazingly, Beatrice sounded convinced. 'Damn, just my luck. Would you be a darling and tell him I called?' Her voice became wry. 'Perhaps he could 'phone me. He does know my number.'

'I'll tell him as soon as he gets back,' Deborah promised. Turning to Oliver as she replaced the receiver she said quietly, 'I hate lying.'

'Sorry.' Oliver poured himself more gin, sounding relieved and unconcerned. 'I couldn't face her.' Deborah stood up finishing her drink. 'She's certainly persistent. Just don't ask me too often,' she said and went to shower.

The water was cold, pelting her body and bringing her back to life. Drying herself she let the towel slip to the marble floor and curiously examined her body in the long rows of mirrored tiles that covered one wall.

Her skin had a golden bloom from the time spent in the sun. Despite her colouring she didn't tan easily.

She was slender, her breasts full, her waist and hips slim, her legs long and well-shaped. The pronounced curves of her body didn't please her. The clothes she designed were for fashionable pencil thin figures and however hard she exercised and dieted, her own body would not conform.

She dried her hair, the long strands blowing against her throat, and left it loose around her shoulders, a long fringe covering her forehead. She made up her face automatically, used to hiding the ravages of inner pain and sleepless nights. She inspected herself for any tell-tale signs as she brushed pale shadow over her eyelids.

Her green eyes were clear and widely-spaced, her nose straight, her mouth generous, hinting at the passionate warmth of her nature. Her jaw was stubborn yet delicate, shaping her face into a heart-shaped triangle. She could never believe she was beautiful, too familiar with features she found frankly boring.

She dressed in a white linen suit with a matching silk blouse, brushed her hair once more, and switched out the lights with a snap.

There was no sign of Oliver, and as they were in plenty of time, she wandered out into the garden. The night had fallen suddenly, warm and black, the sky littered with white stars. Tonight there was no breeze, the hushed air laden with the scent of flowers. Walking around the pool, her high heels clattering on the tiles, to the edge of the garden, she stared down at the town below. The lights were already glowing, twinkling strings of coloured bulbs along the harbour wall.

Melancholy gripped her. She felt as though she had been living in a vacuum for the past three years, hermetically sealed against the power Jake had always held over her. Even her brief marriage and Robert's death had not touched that deep part of her that Jake had reached and which she had locked away at their parting.

Speaking to Tess had released the stopper, letting in the world, letting in Jake, and all those painful memories.

She had loved him so wildly, so completely. Her thoughts halted. *Had* loved him? Was it all in the past? Was it over? She couldn't answer her own questions. There was only confusion if she tried.

The only thing she knew for certain was that she was not free of him. She had tried to cut herself off, but it hadn't worked. And if her feelings for him now weren't love, albeit love twisted by circumstances and deception, what were they? Hate? She couldn't tell, and her head ached from trying.

She *had* hated him when she found Leila in his bed. She had wanted revenge. Her illusions had been shattered and she had wanted to hurt him as he had hurt her. She had been so young then, so innocent. Now she was mature, she had a certain knowledge of the world, a certain sadness at the injustice of life. But there was still part of her that remained untouched. Hope still sprang there refusing to die, and she still yearned for Jake.

'Deborah, are you ready? We'll be late if we don't get a move on.' Oliver's impatient voice drifted out to her on the still air.

'Here,' she called back, moving towards the villa. 'And I've been waiting for you for at least ten minutes.'

They locked the front door and Oliver slipped his arm around her shoulders as they walked to the jeep. He looked young and handsome in a white dinner jacket and dark trousers, his lean body reassuringly hard against her side.

'You look nice.' She smiled up into his face.

He grinned back, pleased. 'I do my best.' Eyeing her from head to toe, he added, 'You look pretty good yourself.'

'What a mutual appreciation society,' Deborah murmured laughing, as they reached the car.

Kerkira was bright and busy, the streets crowded and glowing in the darkness of the night. Strains of music and laughter drifted on the air, and the tantalising scent of food. The hotel was exclusive, a new expensive building on the outskirts of the city. A smart young man stood behind the glass-topped reception desk. He eyed Deborah with discreet admiration as she walked in with Oliver.

'Mr Cole Sullivan's suite, please,' Oliver said with a smile. 'Would you tell him we're here. Mrs Stevens and Mr Lawrence.'

'Of course, sir, right away.' The young man was very efficient, his English perfect.

Cole was waiting to meet them as they stepped out of the lift. 'Honey, you look wonderful,' he said to Deborah, as he kissed her.

'Thank you.' She was very fond of Cole, her green eyes shining as she accepted the compliment.

'Oliver, good to see you,' Cole acknowledged the younger man with a smile, shaking his hand and indicating with a nod that they should enter the suite. 'Can I offer you both a drink? I thought we'd eat up here, a better atmosphere than the restaurant. Janetta is still changing.' His voice held a wry experience of his former wife's habits.

Deborah watched him as he poured the drinks. He was a very attractive man, tall and ruggedly built with cropped dark hair and a roughly hewn face.

His success was stamped all over him, his personality aggressive and pugnacious, yet he was kind and generous to the people he was fond of. Deborah knew he was fond of her. He admired talent and ability, he admired strength of personality. Employees who shrank before him were of no use. He wanted his staff and everybody he came into contact with to stand up for themselves, without fear or particular respect. He was a man of contradictions and Deborah found him fascinating to work with.

Sipping a gin and tonic, she glanced round the air-conditioned suite. It was elegant and comfortable; the walls were peach and white, the carpets incredibly thick, the long sofas flanked by white porcelain lamps. Near the shuttered windows stood a mahogany table set with silver and crystal, white bases making a delightful centrepiece beneath the small chandelier.

Cole and Oliver were chatting about Paleskastritsa but Deborah felt detached from her surroundings, subdued by her thoughts of the past twenty-four hours. Aware that Cole kept glancing at her with a slight frown between his eyes, she picked up an English newspaper from the low mahogany tables in front of her and began to flick through it.

She didn't want to face any questions, and Cole was always so protective, so easily worried about her. He treated her as though she was a piece of china that needed gentle handling. Usually she appreciated his kindness, but tonight she felt she might burst into tears at the slightest show of concern.

She had already read most of the news, her eyes scanning the printed pages quickly, until a headline tucked away at the bottom of a page made her freeze.

'West End playwright in car crash.' The photo

beneath was unmistakably Jake. A publicity shot, she imagined, as she stared at the achingly familiar lines of his face, the wide mobile mouth and cool grey eyes.

Everything inside her seemed to stop shock-still, and for a second she didn't dare to read the print, in case he was ... Her heart began to pound again, sickeningly fast. Dead. Beads of perspiration formed on her forehead. She would have heard if he was dead. She had been listening to the radio while she showered. He was a famous man. They would have reported it. Focusing her eyes with a great effort of will, she forced herself to read on. 'Logan and a woman companion, Caroline Winters, an actress, had been travelling towards London on the motorway when a car skidded across the central reservation and hit them. Miss Winters was shocked but unhurt, Logan suffered two broken ribs. It was a miraculous escape for both of them because the car was a write-off.' Deborah's heart twisted painfully as the words sank in. Caroline Winters. Another beautiful woman, she did not doubt. Jake attracted them so effortlessly. They fell over themselves to get to him.

She looked up at Oliver and Cole but they were still engrossed in conversation. She stared at the photograph of Jake, her body inexplicably weak. Two broken ribs. Was he in hospital?

She swallowed back her gin and tonic trying not to think about the pain she had felt when she thought he might be dead.

'Cole, could I have another drink?' She stood up and he was beside her within a second.

'Sure, honey, same again?' As Deborah nodded, Janetta's voice drifted across.

'Pour one for me, darling, while you're there.'

Deborah turned smiling, all her actions automatic.

Beneath the brilliant smile she was a confused mass of raw nerves.

'Ah, you're ready at last,' Cole remarked with a grin. 'I thought we'd have to start eating without you.'

Janetta ignored that. 'Bourbon and water,' she advised him with a cool smile.

She looked stunning, Deborah thought without envy, in heavy red silk, low off the shoulders with a rustling layered skirt. Around her neck glittered a gold and ruby necklace, complementing the colour of her dress.

They ate near the long windows, the white muslin curtains drifting in the breeze. Silent waiters served the food which was exquisite. There was a clear lemon soup, redolent of fresh herbs, huge shiny peppers stuffed with meat, olives and rice, then slices of veal in a thick creamy sauce. Deborah ate with little appetite. The part of her that was running on automatic was smiling, throwing remarks into the lively conversation around the table. Underneath she felt like a zombie and it was a relief to be able to refuse the rich orange dessert in favour of fresh figs and coffee.

After the meal Janetta somehow persuaded Oliver to dance with her, to the lilting strains of a waltz Cole had found on the radio. Deborah took the opportunity to slip out on to the balcony. The city sprawled below her. The low roar of the traffic assaulting her ears. The balcony was scattered with wrought iron tables and chairs, and terracotta pots of wild roses, and she leant against the rail, enjoying the peace, able to drop her smiling mask. Her solitude was short-lived. Cole came and stood beside her. 'What is it?' he asked quietly.

She was silent for a moment. 'Nothing. I just felt like some air.' Her voice sounded overbright, strained.

She stared at the black sky and wished he would go away.

'Deborah . . .' He paused as though searching for the right words. 'I've been watching you all evening. We go back quite a few years and I know you well enough by now to know that there's something pretty damn serious the matter. Can't you tell me?' He took her arm, turning her to face him, his voice coaxing.

He was right. He did know a lot about her. He knew about Robert, she had needed a shoulder to cry on at the end, and although he knew about Jake, he knew none of the details. She felt she couldn't tell him about it.

'Really Cole, I'm fine. Please, don't worry about me.' She couldn't meet his eyes, her glance resting on the top button of his immaculate white shirt.

His hand still lay along her arm and she realised that they were standing very close. 'We'd better go in, I suppose,' she said lightly.

Cole nodded in silence, and looking up into his eyes, she caught some emotion there that made her step back with shock.

'No . . .' She didn't realise she had spoken.

Cole's mouth twisted self-deprecatingly. 'Oh, Deborah, don't you know?'

Frowning, she asked. 'What?' She had to be sure, even though it might change things for ever.

'I guess you'd run like hell if I told you.' His eyes were serious, but she knew by his voice that he was deliberately trying not to frighten her away.

'Cole . . .' It was totally unexpected and she felt nothing but shocked surprise, and a nagging worry. How could she not have known how he cared for her? How could she have been so stupidly blind?

'Don't say another word.' He dropped his hand, and when she looked uncertainly into his eyes, she saw nothing but his usual friendly cynicism.

'I don't . . . I'm sorry I . . .' She couldn't bear to hurt him, and that, together with her surprise, showed in her face, and Cole sighed.

'Think about it, okay?'

'But . . .'

He held up his hand. 'No, look, I know my timing is lousy—I had no intention of letting you know how I feel. Oh, hell!' He shook his head wryly. 'I don't know about you, but I need a stiff drink.'

'Make that two, I'm dying of thirst after all that dancing.' Janetta's voice was dry, hard-edged. How long had she been standing there near the window, Deborah wondered worriedly. Had she heard everything? Cole merely laughed. 'Serves you damn well right,' he replied, and they all went inside.

Deborah was lost in thought on the way back to the villa. Her head was spinning with the evening's startling events. But, shamefully, her overriding thoughts were of Jake, injured in the car crash.

She closed her eyes and finally accepted that she had to see him again. She had to lay to rest those ghosts that were driving her insane. Time and distance had lent a powerful enchantment. She needed disillusion, the same disillusion she had known when she left him.

'Dammit, I want to go to Tess's party,' she said, turning in her seat to look at Oliver.

'Bravo, my child!' He smiled crookedly, not taking his eyes off the road as he negotiated the narrow streets. 'Being a coward never suited you for a moment.' Deborah forced herself to laugh. It might not have suited her, but it had saved her. She had been safe for three years, and it was going to take more than courage to fling off her protective cloak and face the only man she had ever loved.

CHAPTER THREE

THE weather in London was very cold, the air heavy with fine rain, as they travelled into the city by taxi.

Deborah was quiet, in the grip of an apprehensive foreboding that irritated her.

She had telephoned Tess from the villa. Sealing her doom, she thought melodramatically. Tess had been ecstatic, grateful, which had made Deborah feel even worse.

She didn't know why she was blowing it up out of all proportion. It was only a party, after all. But it was only three days away, looming larger and nearer with every second that ticked by.

She was so engrossed in her own thoughts that she didn't hear what Oliver was saying, surprised when she found herself on the pavement outside their house, her case at her feet, while the taxi carrying Oliver shot away.

Shrugging, she kicked open the gate, picking up her case. The house was tall and thin, a blackened Victorian terraced house near the centre of the city. There was a tiny garden overgrown with wild flowers and worn dipping steps up to the front door.

Originally the house had belonged to Oliver's mother, now it was divided into two spacious flats and shared by Oliver and herself. It had seemed the most sensible solution to the problem of somewhere to live and had proved very satisfactory for both of them.

Inside, the house smelled empty, letters piled up behind the front door. Deborah walked into her flat and switched on the central heating and the kettle. She sorted through the mail, leaving the pile addressed to Oliver on the hall table.

She made some instant coffee, flicking through her own letters, not bothering to open any of them.

After an omelette that she only picked at, she unpacked her case, flinging her dirty clothes into the linen basket. Jake was still pervading the corners of her mind. She didn't want to think about him. She was going to have to focus all her attention on her work now that she was back. Cole was expecting the drawings for her new collection within the month. It wasn't going to be easy.

Tonight the flat felt lonely. It was probably the anti-climax of coming home from holiday, she tried to tell herself, but being back in London brought her nearer to Jake and that made her feel very vulnerable.

The following day her concentration was so poor that she finally gave up all thought of work and decided to travel into the city centre and buy a dress for Tess's party.

She needed something that would boost her confidence and she spent the whole afternoon scouring the West End stores, rejecting without a second glance everything that wasn't perfect.

Her knowledge of design and production made her very critical and it was late in the day when she finally found what she wanted in a small designer boutique just round the corner from Harrods in Knightsbridge.

It was a simple dress in black watermarked silk, beautifully designed with a tight bodice, the back cut away in a deep vee, and a skirt that hugged her hips before falling fluidly to her knees.

She tried it on, knowing it would fit her perfectly, encouraged by the assistant. And of course it did. It

was stunning, and she didn't need the assistant to tell
her that. It lent a pale fire to her blonde hair and a
translucent glow to her skin. There were high-heeled
silk-covered shoes to match, and she emerged from the
shop fifteen minutes later with two gold embossed
bags hanging from her wrist, and a satisfied smile
curving her lips.

Walking down to Harrods on legs that ached from
long hours of pushing through the London crowds,
she bought some gentleman's relish as a small present
for Oliver, then looked around for a taxi.

It was impossible. She had spent longer in town
than she had planned and the rush hour was now in
full swing.

Twenty minutes passed and she must have tried
unsuccessfully to hail at least twenty taxis. She was
feeling worn out and decidedly irritable and could
hardly believe her luck when a black cab suddenly
pulled up in front of her.

Without hesitation she pulled open the door and
climbed inside, freezing into immobility, her parcels
falling from her hands as she came face to face with
the man already inside. It was Jake Logan, the last
person in the world she expected or wanted to see.

She didn't know what to do, she didn't know what
to say, and her heart stopped beating for a second as
she heard his cool greeting.

From somewhere far away she heard her own voice
saying inanely, 'I didn't realise this taxi was occupied.
I——'

'Shut up and sit down. We can share it.' She heard
his clipped instructions to the driver and as the taxi
shot into the heavy traffic, she lost her balance, falling
awkwardly into the seat opposite Jake.

It was like some crazy dream, totally unbelievable.

'Would you mind stopping this taxi?' Her voice was icy, her thoughts spinning in confusion. She didn't dare to look at him. She had glanced at him once when she got in, but since that first shock she had not lifted her eyes.

'Don't be ridiculous, you'll never get another taxi at this time in the afternoon.' His voice was amused, its deep attractive timbre making her shiver inside.

She hadn't heard his voice for three years, but she had never forgotten it, or the effect it always had on her.

'I'll walk. I'd rather anyway,' she gritted, hating his amusement, hating herself for responding.

Jake laughed. 'What's the matter?' he taunted softly, 'Scared? This is a taxi, not a locked bedroom.'

Deborah bit hard on her lower lip, stifling the angry retort that hovered on her tongue. He was laughing at her and she was blind with fury. What was she betraying by making such a fuss about a shared taxi? She didn't dare contemplate what he would read into her panic.

She looked out of the window as the taxi ground to a halt obeying a red light. She would be home in twenty minutes, and how bad could twenty minutes of anything be? All she had to do was keep cool. She lowered her head again, resolving silence, letting the smooth curtain of her hair fall across her flushed cheeks.

She could feel Jake's eyes upon her, intent, staring. There was only a few inches between them in the close confines of the taxi and the air seemed heavy with tension. She looked down at her hands. They were trembling, the knuckles white and she hurriedly pushed them into the pockets of her thick coat, as she tried to cope with the situation she found herself in.

She still felt shocked, incredulous that she was sitting in this taxi with him.

'You haven't changed at all.' Jake's voice broke the silence, low and slightly husky.

Deborah lifted her head, a frown pleating her pale brow. 'Of course I have,' she replied with as much coolness as she could muster. 'Three years is a lifetime.'

'I know.' He gave no emphasis to the words, no expression, yet his voice was loaded with meaning.

Deborah looked out of the dusty window, not bothering to answer, her eyes unfocused, pained.

'How have you been?' He sounded polite now, urbane.

She didn't want to talk and he knew that, she thought furiously.

'Fine.' She had to stop herself snapping, deliberately keeping to one word.

'And your husband?' His gaze narrowed blankly on her averted face.

'He's dead,' she said flatly, regret tightening her mouth.

'So I heard.' He clipped the words harshly, very coolly.

'So why did you ask?' Furiously angry, her eyes met his. Their glances locked, raw electricity flashing between them. Deborah looked into the narrowed silvery grey depths and felt as though she was being sucked into a whirlpool.

'I suppose I was curious to see your reaction,' Jake said very slowly, his eyes still holding hers.

Stunned by his callousness, Deborah swallowed painfully. 'You haven't changed either,' she retorted icily. 'You're still a cold, ruthless swine.'

He acknowledged the insult, his mouth curving in a hard smile. 'And you're still as bad-tempered.'

'Thanks very much.' Strangely the slightest criticism still hurt, and she could feel tears stinging her eyes, blocking her throat as she stared with pretended interest out of the window. But she found herself looking at Jake's reflection, unable to drag her eyes away or focus them on anything beyond the glass.

She had told him the truth, however calculated to insult. He hadn't changed. Perhaps a few more lines etched into the tanned smoothness of his face, but no sign of grey in the vital darkness of his hair. And his body was still magnificent, lean and powerful beneath the expensively tailored dark suit.

She swallowed on the blockage in her throat. He was so near she could feel the pull of his physical magnetism, his sheer strength reaching out to her. She had thought that if, by chance, they ever met again, she would surely be immune. Wasn't time supposed to heal all wounds? How long would she have to wait to be whole again?

The taxi screeched to a sudden halt, horn blaring as another motorist cut out of a narrow side-street in front of them. Deborah fell forward, sliding off the vinyl seat. Strong hands closed around her upper arms, steadying her. And for a second Jake's face was so close to hers that she could see the web of fine lines beneath his eyes, the thickness of black lashes against his skin, before she was gently pushed back into her seat.

The driver was swearing, leaning out of the window to gesticulate. Deborah, unaware of it all, felt her heart pounding in her chest.

'I . . . I'm sorry . . .' She felt the need to break the silence, the awkwardness, her skin running cold with worry.

'It wasn't your fault,' Jake said in a deep quiet voice.

It seemed to her that he hadn't taken his eyes off her since she first stepped into the taxi.

'No . . . I realise that.'

There was a certain stiffness in his posture and she suddenly remembered his broken ribs, the car accident. Had she hurt him, cannoning forward like that? Her heart constricted against her will.

'Do your ribs hurt?' she heard herself asking in a small sympathetic voice.

Jake's eyes held hers, filled with cynical mockery. 'They hurt like hell,' he told her softly, and she knew what he was thinking.

'Looking for sympathy?' she queried coldly.

Jake laughed, a low growl of genuine amusement. 'I'm already basking in your sweet concern, and believe me, I appreciate it.'

Deborah gritted her teeth. 'I just happened to notice it in the newspaper, that's all. Don't imagine I really care. I'm merely trying to make this . . . this ridiculous situation a little more bearable.'

'Really?' Jake's firm mouth curved up at the corners. He looked pleased with himself.

'Yes, really,' Deborah replied, wishing she had held back and not said a word.

'Why so angry, I wonder?' Jake mused wickedly.

Deborah turned away. Why indeed, she wondered, but did not bother to answer him. She felt very close to tears again and she was desperate that he should not see her cry.

'Deborah . . .' He spoke her name deeply, the familiar intonation making her heart turn over. He had already seen her tears.

'No,' she whispered, keeping her head down, not daring to look at him.

'You don't know what I'm going to say,' he teased,

and the gentleness in his voice was almost her undoing. The atmosphere between them had suddenly changed, the air laden with unspoken emotion.

'Jake, please . . .' She could feel herself trembling. 'Please just leave me alone.'

He swore softly under his breath. 'Give me one good reason why I should.' Without warning, he reached out, his long fingers taking her chin, turning her face up to his.

She felt totally exposed as their eyes met, hers brimming with tears, frightened and unsure and slightly defiant.

Jake looked at her with dark intensity, surprised at her vulnerability. She was still so fragile, so easily hurt. She had run from him, disappeared without a word and married another man. And it seemed impossible that he still held the power to hurt her, to make her cry like this.

He released her chin, allowing her the privacy of lowering her eyes again.

'I'm sorry,' he said quietly.

Deborah frowned, swallowing back her tears, wondering at the sudden apology. What had he read in her eyes during those few defenceless seconds?

'Forget it.' In control again, she managed a tight smile, her lashes flickering upwards, not quite daring to look at him.

The moments ticked by in heavy silence. Through her lashes, she watched him remove a slim gold case from his pocket. She watched his hands compulsively. They were strong and tanned, the fingers long, hard-skinned. She remembered their touch against her skin.

'Cigarette?'

His voice made her jump. 'No . . . no thanks,' she stammered in confusion.

'You don't mind if I . . .?'

'Of course not.'

His mouth curved in a slight smile as though he found her abrupt retort amusing. She averted her eyes, thinking that the taxi ride was lasting forever. She heard the flaring of a lighter, and again, that rich aroma of Turkish tobacco.

It was strange how a smell could carry you back into the past, whereas memory could be so deceptive.

'I hear you're working for Cole Sullivan.' He was deliberately trying to lighten the atmosphere, and Deborah, stiff and over-suspicious, wondered at his motive.

'Yes.' Her one word answer was deliberately uncooperative.

'Do you enjoy it?' He was not to be put off. She heard the teasing amusement in his voice.

'Yes, I enjoy it.' At the thought of Cole and that last dinner in Corfu, faint colour stole into her cheeks, and although she tried to hide it, she was well aware that Jake had seen it.

Through the haze of fragrant smoke that veiled his hard face she could see the narrowing of his eyes.

'Look, do we have to talk?' she demanded coldly, so exposed she felt as though her skin had been ripped away.

Jake smiled, and she couldn't read his expression. 'What are you so scared of?'

'You,' she replied with bald honesty and regretted it immediately.

'Why?' He shot the question back expressionlessly.

'I don't know.' It was an unsteady half-truth.

Jake sighed, about to say something, changing his mind.

Deborah fiddled with the gold bangle on her wrist,

trying to work out the answer to his question. The very sight of him made her heart beat violently, that was frightening enough. He seemed so untouched, as though he had forgotten they had ever been lovers, as though she was a stranger.

His voice broke into her reverie. 'Tess tells me that you've accepted her invitation to the party.'

Deborah nodded. She wished now that she hadn't and it showed in her eyes. She could not have imagined how traumatic it would be, meeting Jake face to face again.

'Yes, of course. It would have been churlish to refuse just because of . . .' She shrugged, fighting for composure.

'Because of us?' Jake completed the sentence for her, his hard mouth mocking.

'If you like.' She didn't like the admission. She pulled the collar of her coat higher around her throat. Jake watched the movement, the shaking fingers. 'Cold?' he taunted in a low voice.

'What do you think?' She couldn't help snapping, tension evident in every line of her slender body.

'I think, for Tess's sake, we should seem to be getting along with each other,' Jake said expressionlessly.

Deborah stared. 'Is that what this is all about?' she demanded unsteadily, suddenly realising that this meeting had been planned. She should have remembered that Jake left nothing to chance. Pride stiffened her spine. 'Well, you can rest assured that I won't upset Tess in any way at all. I'm looking forward to seeing her, actually.'

'And she you,' Jake responded with a smile. Then with heartfelt relief, Deborah felt the taxi pulling to a halt and glancing out of the window, found herself in front of her own house. At last.

She fumbled in her bag for her purse, wanting to pay for her share of the taxi. Ridiculous though it was, she couldn't bear the thought of being in debt to him, however small the amount was.

'Forget it,' he said, reading her clumsy actions.

'No, I can't ...' Her fingers wouldn't work. She couldn't open her purse.

'Deborah, I said forget it.' There was amusement in his voice but a warning, too.

'I ... I ...' Defeated, she reached for the door handle and clambered out. 'Thank you——'

She felt gauche and so foolish. What was the matter with her? Trembling, tongue-tied, unable to express herself in any way at all, she felt like a shy adolescent, faced in the flesh with some long-loved idol.

'The pleasure is mine.' He smiled though his eyes were serious, unreadable.

She turned away, nearly bolting through the gate, diving into her handbag again for the doorkeys. The sky was darkening, a light flurry of snow beginning to fall, as the winter evening drew in. The street lights gave off their all-pervading orange glare and it was so cold that her breath hung on the air in a wide cloud. Her handbag seemed suddenly bottomless, filled with unnecessary rubbish and she couldn't find her keys anywhere.

She was waiting, listening for the noise of the taxi drawing away and the longed-for knowledge that Jake had gone. And she almost jumped out of her skin when a hand gently touched her shoulder. She whirled around to find him only inches away, towering over her, tall and powerful and somehow menacing.

'You forgot these.' He held out the two carrier bags that held her new dress and shoes.

'Oh——' She took them from him, electricity burning her as their fingers brushed. 'Thanks.'

'What's the matter?' Jake asked, staring at her again.

'I—nothing, I don't know what you mean.'

His mouth tightened impatiently. 'Why are you so damned afraid of me?'

'I'm not.' She drew herself up, her green eyes meeting his with defiance.

'Have dinner with me tonight, then?' he said with a smile.

Dumbfounded, Deborah shook her head. 'I already have plans for this evening,' she managed shakily.

'Tomorrow?' There was a silky mockery in his voice as though he knew she would refuse.

'No.' She pushed a hand through her hair, feeling the wetness of snow clinging there.

'Why not?'

'Why are you asking me?' she countered, her knees trembling at the persuasive charm in his face.

'Isn't it obvious?'

'No, otherwise ...' Her voice trailed off as she looked into his eyes, her heart lurching at what she read there. It could not be translated into words or thoughts. It was pure emotion and it demanded response.

'What do you want from me?' she whispered, suddenly frightened. 'Why are you doing this?'

'I want to make some kind of contact with you. I want to get through that wall of ice you've built around yourself,' Jake replied grimly. 'I want to know why you're frozen up inside. I want to know what happened to the woman I knew.'

Deborah laughed bitterly. How could he be so blind? How could he not know that if she was frozen behind a wall of ice, it was all his fault?

'I'm surprised you even remember.'

'Oh, I remember.' His voice was low, shivering through every nerve in her body. 'I remember everything, every moment we spent together.'

'That was years ago,' she retorted, still trembling violently. 'It's all over now, and after Tess's party we won't see each other again, so let's just leave it at that, shall we?'

'Do you really believe that?' Jake asked, surveying her through narrowed eyes.

Deborah bit her lip, betraying her anxiety. 'I don't understand . . .'

'No, you don't, do you?' he said calmly and she heard him laughing as she turned her head away.

The snow was falling heavily now, whirling down from the impenetrable darkness above. Neither of them noticed. She still hadn't found her keys, but she had the feeling that if she opened the front door, Jake would be inside before she had time to stop him. She didn't want that.

'Obviously not. So why don't you tell me?' she answered coolly, wanting him to go. She didn't know what to say to him and she could not bear to look at him. Her nerves were stretched as tight as wire.

Jake's long fingers closed around her chin, tilting back her head and forcing her to meet the probing depths of his eyes.

She struggled, her breath locked in her lungs, but he was far too strong for her. She couldn't move an inch beneath the strength of those fingers.

He watched her impotent struggling, gazing into her pale face with cool intensity. 'Don't fight me, Deborah,' he warned softly. 'You can't win, so don't back yourself into a corner. I never lose, as any number of people who have tried to take me on could tell you.' He lifted his other hand, gently stroking back the wet hair from her forehead.

'Thanks for the warning.' She tried to make her voice acid but it only came out shakily.

Jake smiled again and said too smoothly. 'It's not a warning, Deborah, it's a promise.'

He released his grip on her chin and turning on his heel, walked away into the darkness.

CHAPTER FOUR

THE days sped by with supernatural speed and the day of Tess's party dawned all too soon.

Deborah woke that morning with a headache, a dull pain throbbing in her temples.

She hadn't slept well, a nervous anxiety in her stomach keeping her tossing and turning all night, but after a shower, a cup of strong black coffee and two aspirins, she felt a little more human.

She dressed in tight denim jeans and a thick baggy pink sweater, still clutching her cup of coffee as she wandered into the lounge.

It was a high-ceilinged room, the walls ragged cream. An old Persian carpet—a present from Oliver, lay on the polished wooden floorboards, and between the two high windows with their wooden shutters, stood her two work desks cluttered with books and drawings, brushes and pens.

It was a perfect room for working in because the windows faced the north, their cold, demanding light suitable for the colours she had to match in her designs.

She sipped her coffee slowly, the pile of work on the desks somehow accusing her. She'd hardly done a thing since returning from Corfu and Cole was already making noises about the new collection. She was going to be very busy over the next week or so. As well as the designs Cole had already made a number of appointments for her. When it came to business, he was as hard as nails and he wouldn't take any excuses.

She had never been the victim of his sharp tongue, but she had heard him tearing into other people who had dared to be inefficient, and it had scared the living daylights out of her. She really would have to get on with some work. Perhaps it would even take her mind off Jake.

The doorbell rang as she moved towards the cluttered desk and she half smiled, realising that she was glad of the diversion.

Oliver wouldn't be up yet, it was far too early, and besides, she had heard him coming in last night. He had sounded pretty drunk, kicking the empty milk bottles down the steps as he staggered through the front door. Deborah had given him two cups of strong black coffee and left him to it, exasperated and a little saddened by his helplessness.

She ran downstairs as the bell rang again. Outside stood a delivery man with an armful of deep red roses, their heavy scent mingling with the cold morning air.

'Mrs Deborah Stevens?' The young man smiled.

Deborah nodded, staring, and the flowers were thrust into her hands. It seemed as though there were hundreds of them, transporting her back to the summer. She knew who they were from without reading the attached card, although she tried to tell herself that they might be from Cole, or even an unknown admirer.

She was pushing the front door shut with her foot, when Beatrice arrived. Still stunned by the flowers, the older woman was in the hall before Deborah could say a word.

'My, you must be popular. And a rich man too, by the look of it—hot house roses at this time of year,' Beatrice remarked, raising her delicate eyebrows as she watched Deborah struggling with the flowers.

'You'd think so, wouldn't you?' Deborah's voice was dry. Popular was not the word she would have chosen herself, she thought, as she surveyed the other woman.

As always, Beatrice looked fantastic, her dark hair gleaming in a smooth chignon, her pale face flawlessly made up. Her long boots were light leather, matching her woollen skirt and fur trimmed woollen coat.

'Is Oliver around?' Beatrice moved towards his internal front door.

'I don't think he's up yet.' Deborah stepped forward, worried.

'I'll wake him up, then,' Beatrice smiled, shutting the door behind her as she stepped inside, leaving Deborah alone in the hall.

Oliver might be angry, but it was his own fault, she decided as she climbed the stairs. Beneath that cool beauty, Beatrice hid a quick determined mind. If she wanted Oliver, he would have to sort it out for himself. There was nothing Deborah could do.

Back in her flat, she carefully put down the roses and picked up the attached envelope. Inside, a small card had one word scrawled across it in strong black handwriting. Jake.

She stared at it, feeling again his presence, his strength. Why had he sent her flowers? Why had he asked her to have dinner with him?

The hairs on the back of her neck prickled with worry. She couldn't begin to fathom his motives.

The loud rapping on the door made her jump. It was Oliver, pale and bleary, hastily dressed, his feet bare.

'Have you got any coffee?' he demanded, walking in.

Deborah frowned at him. 'In the kitchen.'

He padded towards the door, re-emerging moments later with a bowl full of coffee beans.

'Very neat. I can't find a bloody thing in my kitchen.'

'Too many empty bottles?' Deborah enquired sarcastically, still staring at the flowers.

Oliver pulled a face. 'Very witty. What's the matter with you this morning?'

Beneath his drowsy pallor, Deborah could see that he was excited, elated.

It was Beatrice who had brought him back to life. Deborah knew how his mind worked. Beatrice had come to see him, she had actually made the effort to come to the flat. And to Oliver, trapped by love he could not fight, that seemed to prove some sort of caring.

'There's nothing the matter with me,' she said, smiling at him because she couldn't bear to spoil that elation.

'You look worn out,' Oliver told her bluntly, only noticing the roses as he walked towards the door. 'Who are they from?'

'It's none of your business, and besides, Beatrice will be waiting for you,' she said sweetly.

'Okay, okay. You'll tell me in your own good time,' Oliver sounded confident. 'See you later.'

'I won't be counting on it,' she replied, as she shut the door behind him, and heard him laughing as he ran downstairs.

Refusing to think too deeply, she scouted round for vases and finally filled five with the roses. Their scent and colour filled the flat, vivid and redolent of sunny afternoons.

She made herself more coffee and stood by the window, all thought of work forgotten. A light snow shower had coated the roofs, and had already turned to slush in the street. It was cold, a misty winter morning, the weather uncharacteristically bad for March. She sipped her coffee slowly, enjoying the bitter flavour, and watched two sparrows fighting in the garden opposite.

She was trying to think about work, but she could only think of Jake. He had exploded back into her life again, leaving her breathless and confused.

And there was still the party to face before she could start avoiding him again. She could hardly believe she was the same person who had become his lover in the green summer beauty of Windermere, three years ago.

After those two weeks of sheer perfection, when she was due home, Jake had driven her back to London, her paintings and empty sketchbooks neatly packed into the boot of his car.

Somehow things had changed from then on. Back in the bustle of the city and the daily routine, those brief weeks in the Lake District became hazy and unreal.

She no longer had Jake to herself. He had to work and he had commitments that he could not break. Because she had been so wildly in love with him, she had been jealous of those commitments. Looking back, she knew she had been very unreasonable, unable to help herself.

She remembered her first visit to his house. She met Tess and Leila there. Tess had been friendly and curious, but Leila had eyed Deborah with sullen hostility, making her position clear right from the start.

'Don't worry about Leila,' Tess had said cheerfully. It was a hot afternoon and they had been sitting on the bank of the river that ran through the garden of the house, dangling their feet in the cool clear water. 'She has terrible moods, but I'm sure she doesn't mean to be nasty.'

Secretly, Deborah had wondered. It was obvious that Leila had hated her right from the start. She did not bother to hide or deny it. Except when Jake was there. Then she had eyes only for him.

'Is she related to you?' Deborah had asked.

'She's an orphan,' Tess had revealed surprisingly. 'I think she might be a very distant relation. Jake brought her back from France to live with us. He's so kind, and Leila dotes on him now.'

Deborah had already noticed that, and although she didn't want to she'd felt the first faint stirrings of jealousy.

She had tried to like Leila, for Jake and for Tess, but she couldn't. And in the end, she had hated her; hated her dark sullen beauty and malicious tongue.

Her jealousy had driven a wedge between her and Jake, even though Leila's name hardly ever came up in conversation.

Deborah had been very young, insecure and over-sensitive, hardly able to believe that she could inspire love in a hard sophisticated man like Jake.

She remembered little things that Leila said, tiny jibes, seemingly innocent double-edged remarks that got right under her skin like splinters of rotten wood. She would wake in the middle of the night, remember them, and spend hours worrying, wondering, undermined by Leila's cunning.

She had never known jealousy before, but she was experiencing its destructive powers to the full. It was blinding her thoughts and her judgment.

She was seeing another side of Jake, too. During that summer, Robert was back in London and Deborah spent a day with him. She hadn't seen him for ages because he was studying aviation at an American college.

They spent the day touring the sights of London, chatting about old times. He was kind and amusing. They had been friends since childhood, same schools, same lifestyle. Robert and his mother had lived next door to Deborah for most of her life. Before Oliver, Robert had always taken care of her, protected her from the neighbourhood bullies, never hiding his affection.

When he drove her back to her flat late that night, she did not notice the low silver car parked on the other side of the road. Robert escorted her to the front door, taking her by surprise, pulling her into his arms and kissing her passionately.

It was the first time he had ever kissed her in a sexual way and shock held her passive in his embrace.

When he finally released her, she looked up into his eyes and found an expression there that disturbed her. She hadn't guessed that he might feel any differently than her. She was fond of him, loved him like a brother, but that was all.

Her obvious shock had embarrassed him. She heard him mumbling something about 'phoning her the following day, then he was gone.

Still struggling with surprise, Deborah opened the front door and stepped inside, gasping as a hand grabbed her shoulder. She was roughly pulled round and found herself face to face with Jake, his grey eyes as cold and as dangerous as steel.

'Jake . . .' She smiled uncertainly, glad to see him.

He did not speak, merely pushed her inside and into her flat, violently kicking the door shut with his foot.

She turned to face him, still not understanding, her

·mouth curved in a soft smile.

Jake's eyes narrowed, his face a cold ruthless mask. 'Where the hell have you been?' he demanded tautly.

'Out to dinner . . .' she stammered, afraid of him for the first time. He was so big and powerful, his anger almost tangible.

'Who is he?' Jake bit the words out fast and clear and furious.

'Robert?' It sounded inane. She felt herself trembling, her eyes enormous as she looked at him. 'He's a friend.'

'Friend?' He threw the word back at her contemptuously, his mouth hard. She heard him swearing under his breath. He was looking at her as though he wanted to hit her, his body tense, his hands curled into fists at his sides. He was hard and dangerous, and her heart began to thump painfully.

'Yes, he's a friend . . . I . . .'

'And dinner took until now?' He cut off her explanation mid-sentence, staring at her with violent probing eyes.

Deborah looked at her watch. It was one-thirty. She hadn't realised how late it was. 'I didn't realise . . .' She spoke unintentionally, giving herself away.

'I'd be waiting?' He took a step towards her and she shrank away terrified. 'I can believe that, you cold-hearted little bitch.'

'You're frightening me,' she whispered, shivering as though she was freezing cold.

She felt guilty even though she wasn't. Jake could see that too. He had seen Robert kissing her. The knowledge lay in every taut line of his body. He had seen it all and he believed the worst, because the guilt in her eyes kept making a liar of her.

'Nothing happened,' she whispered, staring

nervously down at her feet, because her eyes, so easily read by Jake, seemed to be damning her.

'I saw him touching you,' Jake muttered through clenched teeth, as though the mere thought was unendurable.

'Don't . . .' Terrified by the depth of his jealousy, the darkness in his eyes, she moved further away. 'You're frightening me,' she said again.

'I'll teach you to be really frightened if I find you with him again,' Jake said hoarsely. 'Is he your lover? Is he?'

She didn't answer, unable to say a word. He moved towards her, silent and furious, like a tiger ready for the kill, his mouth hardening as she shrank back against the wall.

His hands closed on her shoulders, their pressure bruising. He shook her until she felt loose and limp. 'Answer me,' he grated harshly. 'Is he your lover?'

Deborah swallowed on the blockage of tears in her throat, and wordlessly shook her head, her wide eyes holding his.

Jake groaned deep in his throat. She heard that groan and shuddered, then his mouth was on hers, hard and erotic, punishing, as though he didn't care that he hurt her. His hands still bruised her shoulders, the strength of his fingers possessive and ruthless, but Deborah's response was as violent and overwhelming as the blind anger that drove him.

Her lips moved under his, gentle and pleading with desire. She felt the quickening of his heart beneath her shocked fingers, and wanted him, loved him too much to protest at his furious behaviour.

As the kiss deepened, her hands slid up over his wide shoulders to tangle in the darkness of his hair, stroking greedily.

Jake shuddered, his anger dissolving in raw unconcealed hunger. His own hands left her shoulders, pulling her body against his, both arms around her. They ended up in her narrow bed, their lovemaking white hot, restless with desperation.

It always happened that way. Jake's possessive fury, the dark streak beneath his cool charm, would surface from nowhere, if she even looked at somebody else. His obsessiveness terrified her. And she had loved him so much that it had broken her heart.

'You're mine, dammit,' he told her once. 'You belong to me. And I won't let anyone else near you. Do you understand?'

It hurt that he did not trust her after that episode with Robert. She felt as though she would never know him. She could not understand that darkness in him, the terrible jealousy that engulfed him in anger whenever she looked at another man. Perhaps it was the turbulence of his upbringing, the harshness of his life, that had produced this need to possess totally. He was so unlike any other man she had met before. He lived by his own rules, and it showed in the untamed compulsive strength of his face, in every sleek movement of his body. He defied convention and the rules by which ordinary people lived their lives. And his plays held a wisdom, a deep perception of the world around him, a knowledge of motive and thought.

Looking back, she saw that she had been far too young, barely out of school. How could she possibly have hoped to get to know, to understand, a man of the world like Jake. Surely that had been doomed from the start. Every detail of her own disillusionment was still starkly clear in her mind. She remembered creeping into his bedroom at the house, pressing her face to his pillow. How childish that seemed now. And she remembered the faint smell of perfume clinging to the pillowcases.

It rose in her throat now, choking her. A rich sickly perfume, cloying and exotic. A perfume she would never have dreamed of wearing herself.

She had not been suspicious at the time. In fact, she had forgotten all about it, until two weeks later, when she arrived unexpectedly at the house, hoping to surprise Jake.

She saw herself in slow motion, running up the stairs, imagining that he must still be in bed. It was very early and the rest of the house was deserted.

As she reached the bedroom, she heard the hissing of the shower. She pushed open the door, calling his name, the words dying on her lips as she saw Leila in his bed. Leila, with her cloudy black hair billowing over Jake's pillows, her smooth bare shoulders rising from the silk sheets.

The shower hissed on against Deborah's chaotic thoughts, as it all became painfully clear.

How stupid she was, not to have realised. Leila had been too hostile from the start. She was smiling now though, a cruel triumphant deriding smile. As though she was glad that Deborah had caught her in such a compromising position.

And the perfume, that sweet exotic scent seemed to fill the room, choking Deborah with the realisation that this affair between Leila and Jake had been going on for some time.

Suddenly her limbs had started to work again, and without a word she had turned and run like the wind down the stairs and out of the house. She had driven back to her flat far too fast and once behind the front door, she had cried her heart out.

That had been the end as far as she was concerned. She had closed in on herself, feeling as though there was something broken inside her.

Oliver had found her, late in the evening, huddled on the sofa, still crying.

Without meaning to, she told him everything.

'I don't want to see him ever again,' she had muttered hysterically against his shoulder. 'Not ever.'

'You don't have to,' Oliver had replied soothingly. 'You don't have to do anything you don't want to.'

'But if he comes round . . .'

'I'll speak to him, don't worry.'

'But I don't want him to know that I saw . . .' Her voice was high, fretful.

'Leave it to me.' Oliver had stroked her hair, soothed her.

For some reason, that had been her worst fear, seeing him again. The pain had been so bad, she had wanted to die.

Jake had come round the next day. Perhaps he had been telephoning her. The telephone had rung several times during the afternoon. She had not answered it. She heard the doorbell ring and did not move. She felt numb, detached. She heard the voices downstairs as Oliver waylaid him, lying, saying she was out.

She heard the harshness, the violence in Jake's voice, and shuddered, pressing her hands to her ears.

Jake had known she was there. She felt it, heard it in his voice. Luckily Cole had been downstairs at the time, negotiating the sale of a painting from Oliver. He helped evict Jake from the house. Oliver would never have been able to do it on his own. Jake was too physically powerful, aware of his own strength.

Deborah crouched in the darkness near the door, a fist pressed to her mouth, feeling sick to her stomach.

She could hear almost every word from downstairs and her mind was filled with the image of Leila in Jake's bed.

Finally Jake left, and she could not help herself moving over to the window. She watched from behind the blinds, jumping with fright as he turned at the gate to look up at her window.

He can't see me, she thought hysterically, but he seemed to be looking straight at her, his eyes silvered with a bitter deadly anger. She watched him slide into his car, the engine roaring angrily into life, the tyres squealing in protest as he shot away. She stared out into the night and started to cry again.

Oliver came up fifteen minutes later, his face pale, nervous. He switched on the lights and made coffee for them both in her tiny kitchen, pushing aside her protests that she didn't want any.

'My God,' he said, sitting down beside her. 'He scared the wits out of me.'

Deborah was silent for a moment. 'I'm sorry.'

'I thought he was going to kill me when I told him you didn't want to see him any more. He's crazy.'

Deborah sipped her coffee without noticing what she was doing. It was dark and bitter and it burnt her tongue. 'I can't stay here,' she muttered dazedly.

Oliver looked at her, frowning. 'If you mean that, I can help. And I think you should get away, because I don't think he'll let you go easily. The man is a maniac.'

Despite all that had happened, Deborah wanted to defend Jake, but she bit back the words, angry with herself. It wasn't Oliver's fault, after all.

'How can you help?' she asked instead.

The following evening she had dinner in Oliver's flat. Cole was there. She felt embarrassed as they were introduced, hardly able to meet his eyes. But he mentioned nothing of the previous evening's events.

She liked him right away. He was kind and charming, and seeing her portfolio, he offered her a job. She had grabbed it with both hands. A week later she was in Los Angeles, Cole having sorted out all the official documentation with a minimum of fuss.

Robert was ecstatic that she was in America. His college was in San Diego, only a short plane ride from Los Angles.

He would turn up at the apartment Cole had rented for her, usually at the weekend, and by gentle and persistent persuasion, urge her to have dinner with him.

She found it difficult to refuse. She had no excuses to offer anyway. She locked away her terrible pain, slowly learning to face the world with a facade of cool amusement that betrayed nothing of her inner thoughts or feelings.

Robert was good company. He was kind and reassuring and he helped to bring her out of herself. She didn't allow him to kiss her again though. She kept him at a very safe distance, making it clear that she wanted no romantic involvement.

Until one night, out of the blue, Robert asked her to marry him. The proposal shocked her and she turned him down as gently as she possibly could, her heart aching because there was no way she could not hurt him. He loved her, could not conceal it any longer and she knew what hell unrequited love could be.

The following day, the small plane he was co-piloting on a test flight, crashed on take-off.

Robert was seriously injured, unconscious for more than twenty-four hours. Frances, his mother, flew out immediately to be at his bedside and it was she who contacted Deborah.

'He's regained consciousness, thank God,' she said on the telephone, her voice full of choking tears. 'And he's asking for you over and over again. Please come.'

The pleading quality in her voice had Deborah on the next available flight to San Diego.

She couldn't stop wondering if the accident was her fault, a terrible guilt seeping through her mind, even though she found out later that it was a mechanical fault, something to do with the plane, not an error of judgment.

Both Robert and Frances had been pathetically glad to see her when she arrived at the hospital, but she soon realised, to her horror, that Frances was under the impression that Deborah and Robert were engaged.

She tried to explain that it wasn't true, that she had, in fact, turned down Robert's proposal, but Frances burst into tears, terribly upset.

She learned later from the doctor that Robert was suffering from slight amnesia. He couldn't remember the crash, or the preceding forty-eight hours. It was quite usual, the doctor pointed out, when she talked to him.

'However, his improvement has been marked since your arrival, Miss Lawrence.' She had remembered those words ever since. The doctor was tall and fair, his face permanently creased with worry. His manner was calm and soothing. 'But he's still hovering between life and death. Frankly I believe you're the only reason he's hanging on.'

Deborah had stayed with Frances, comforting her as well as she could. Robert's recovery was very slow and very painful, often there was no progress at all. His amnesia remained as well.

Frances exerted pressure, and tried to persuade Deborah to marry Robert. Deborah recognised it, but couldn't blame her. Robert was her only son and they were very close.

She resisted for a while, but Frances's anxiety worried her. The older woman had shed pounds and pounds since the accident. She looked much older, her nerves shattered, her face tense as she paced around the hospital chain-smoking, despite the no-smoking signs.

Those weeks at the hospital in San Diego seemed to drag on for ever. Cole was wonderful, giving her as much time off as she needed. Jake's betrayal still burned in her mind, but there was plenty to occupy her conscious thoughts.

All of a sudden, Robert's recovery halted and the days were filled with a new anxiety as Deborah finally reached her decision.

Despite his weak protests, she married him at his bedside two weeks later. Frances's grateful face almost made her cry, and when she looked at Robert she knew she was doing the right thing.

The doctor now gave him only a few months. His injuries were too severe and he was still very weak. It was heartbreaking news, but Robert was happy, and in a strange way Deborah could share that.

She would sit by his bed all day, her eyes full of affection and they would talk for hours, holding hands. She felt glad that she'd married him because it obviously meant so much to him.

Three months later, he died peacefully in his sleep. Deborah felt numb. It seemed as though everyone she had ever cared for had been taken away from her.

Back in London, a month or two after the funeral, she was buying some fruit, and absent-mindedly walked out of the shop without her change.

The assistant, who she knew quite well, called after her. 'Mrs Stevens, your change.'

Deborah turned, smiling and found herself face to face with Jake. She hadn't seen him for months and now he had come from nowhere. He was staring down at her with a bleak bitter anger burning in his eyes.

Her smile died on her lips and she stared back, unable to break the eye contact.

He did not say a word, his silence trapping her. She gazed up into his familiar hard-boned face, and felt herself shaking inside. She couldn't stop looking at him.

Jake finally broke the silence, his glance dropping to her left hand, where a thin gold band circled her wedding finger. She had not bothered to remove it after Robert died. She had forgotten she was still wearing it.

'Mrs Stevens,' he repeated and the words sounded curious on his lips, harsh and contemptuous. Deborah realised with a tiny flash of shock, that he had not known about her marriage.

'Yes,' she replied shakily, his obvious derision cutting her to ribbons, and forcing her to pull herself together, to lie for self-protection. 'You didn't know?'

Jake's mouth hardened into a cruel line. He looked at her, as though he wanted to kill her. 'That poor fool you were seeing, I suppose,' he drawled, with a smile that came nowhere near the ice in his eyes.

It was too close to the truth and Deborah flinched.

'Drop dead,' she muttered, turning away, unable to bear any more. She almost ran from him, tears suddenly scalding her eyes. But she couldn't miss his cynical 'good luck,' as she rushed blindly into the street . . .

The telephone was ringing, bringing her back to the present to notice that the room had darkened around her. There was only the orange glare of the street lights, softening the furniture into unknown shadows.

She picked up the receiver, still lost in memory, her hand shaking in case it was Jake. It wasn't.

'How about dinner tonight?' Cole's voice travelled down the line, making her jump.

'Cole . . .' She was confused for a moment, as the invitation sank in.

'Deborah, are you okay?'

'Yes, yes, of course.' She snapped on the lamp that stood on the desk, blinking in the glare. 'Dinner? No, I'm sorry, I can't make it tonight.'

'Date?' Cole asked casually.

'No, a party. An old friend—it's her twenty-first,' Deborah explained. 'I'm sorry——'

'Hey, don't apologise.' Cole sounded relieved.

Because she didn't have a date? She remembered Corfu and frowned. That was something else she would have to sort out. 'Okay, I won't.' She made her voice sound bright and easy. 'But you'll have to find someone else to keep you company. Has Janetta gone back to New York?'

Cole snorted expressively. 'Yes, thank God. That woman is like an alligator, she's after my blood. Why the hell do you think I'm back in London?'

'Don't be mean!' Deborah protested, but she was laughing, because she could see what he meant.

'You weren't married to her,' Cole said, laughing too. 'Anyway, enjoy yourself tonight, sweetheart. And don't forget, you're seeing that client in Kendal tomorrow—so lay off the booze.'

'Yes, sir!' She *had* forgotten about driving up to Kendal. It had completely slipped her mind. She wasn't looking forward to the long drive up north.

As she replaced the receiver, the smile faded from her lips. She glanced at her watch and saw that it was well after seven. The party was an hour away and she felt like crying her eyes out.

CHAPTER FIVE

THEY were leaving for Tess's party at eight-thirty, which left Deborah just under an hour to get ready.

She ran a bath quickly, her party mood non-existent. She felt miserable, heavy with memories of the past, and the thought of coming face to face with Jake again didn't improve her mood.

She lay in the scented water, trying to tell herself that she would cope. She wasn't a naïve, unsophisticated teenager any more. Three years ago, Jake had smiled and demanded everything, and she had handed it all to him on a plate. She would have done anything for him.

Grimacing with self-derision she shampooed her hair. Once made, such mistakes could never be undone. There was no chance to wipe the slate clean and begin again. Foolishly she had expected fidelity from Jake, when he had never promised it. When she had realised that Leila was his mistress, she had hated him, burning for revenge.

She rinsed her hair, tugging her fingers through the wet weight of it. How did she feel about him now? The need for revenge had faded, but she still hated him, feared him, mistrusted him. And she didn't want to see him again.

She stepped out of the bath, gazing at her naked body as she reached for a towel. No man had touched her since Jake. He had been her first and only lover. Unbidden, the memory of his hands against her skin, his mouth touching her breasts, rose in her mind. She shivered, her body aching with sudden need. She bit her lip hard, turning from the mirror. Perhaps tonight she would meet a lover, someone to exorcise Jake from her body and from her mind. Perhaps.

She dressed with care after drying her hair and brushing it until it shone like a golden halo around her face. She applied her make-up with all the skill she could muster. She needed a mask of confidence, something to hide behind. When she was finally ready, she knew she looked good.

The black dress was perfect, well worth the extravagance, and as a final touch, she clipped back her golden hair at the nape of her neck with an ebony comb. With one last look in the mirror, she left the bedroom and collected her fur cape, her handbag and the slim gold bracelet she had bought for Tess.

She wandered round the flat, switching off lights and closing doors and was ready when Oliver arrived. He whistled under his breath as she opened the door. 'You look fantastic. Pulled out all the stops, eh?'

'Very perceptive,' she retorted with a smile, but she locked the door with fingers that wouldn't stop shaking.

Oliver watched her, frowning slightly as though he had only just realised how much courage it was going to take for her to attend this party.

'Don't worry,' he said, slipping his arm around her shoulders as they walked downstairs. 'I'll stick close by you.'

Deborah turned to look at him, taking in the gleaming smoothness of his hair and the immaculate darkness of his dinner jacket and trousers. 'Does it show that much?'

'Only to me.'

Stepping out into the cold night air, Deborah knew

that if Oliver could see her nervousness, then Jake certainly would.

'You won't leave me alone, will you?' she begged, knowing she was being foolish.

Oliver promised but as they sped out of London towards Jake's house, the promise held little consolation or comfort.

They arrived too soon, even though the house was some distance from London.

Oliver pulled off the road through high wrought iron gates, flanked by huge stone lions, and down a rhododendron-lined drive.

Deborah looked at the house as they approached it, her heart turning over. It was still exactly the same, though she hadn't been here for three years—a huge late Georgian house, half covered with climbing ivy.

Oliver parked next to a grey Rolls Royce, smiling wryly as he pulled to a halt. The front of the house was lined with rows of cars. The imposing front door was wide open, the warmth of light and music spilling out into the silent night.

Deborah slid out of the car, pulling her cape tighter round her body. It was colder here in the country, the sky that thick impenetrable black that is never seen in the city. She stood looking round, not wanting to go inside, glad that Oliver was still locking the car. He might not be here, she kept telling herself, trying to hold her fear at bay. Somewhere far away an owl hooted and the trees whispered in the cold wind.

'Ready?' Oliver was beside her, taking her arm. He was smiling and she knew why. Those expensive cars spoke of money and influence, perhaps a commission. A lot of Oliver's work came out of social introductions.

'You mercenery,' she said under her breath, as they walked towards the house.

Oliver laughed, about to reply when Tess appeared, framed in the glowing light from the doorway.

'Deborah! I thought it was you when the car drew up. I've been waiting for you. And Oliver, how are you? Oh, it's so lovely to see you both again. Come in.' She rushed forward, not pausing for breath, pulling them inside, enclosing them in warmth and welcome.

'It's lovely to see you, too,' Deborah found herself smiling despite her shaking nerves. 'You look beautiful,' she added, leaning forward to kiss the younger girl's cheek. She meant it. Tess looked stunning in a candy-striped ball dress. Tightly ruched from breast to hip, leaving her shoulders bare, it flared out to her knees. Her dark hair was scraped back into a shining knot on the top of her head, leaving the delicate bone structure of her face exposed. Around her throat lay a glittering diamond necklace.

She saw Deborah looking at it, and reached up to touch it. 'Jake's present,' she explained with excited eyes. 'Isn't it fantastic?'

'Mmm, gorgeous.' The mention of Jake's name made Deborah's heart miss a beat. Was he here? Tess had given her an opportunity to voice the casual question but she couldn't bring herself to ask it, and the moment passed.

'Shall I take your coat? Come upstairs, you can freshen up in my room.' Tess turned to Oliver. 'Will you be——?'

He cut her off mid-sentence. 'Run along children, and talk,' he laughed, already moving towards the music.

Tess giggled and whisked Deborah up the wide staircase to her bedroom.

'I was so afraid you wouldn't come,' she confided,

watching as Deborah discarded her cape and began fiddling with her hair.

'We weren't planning to come back from Corfu until next week,' Deborah replied, staring at her reflection in a large mahogany-framed mirror.

'So I dragged you away from all that sunshine,' Tess said laughingly, not sounding at all repentant.

'I did want to come,' Deborah admitted. 'But . . .'

'I know. I said some terrible things to you,' Tess cut in, misunderstanding.

Deborah pushed her hair behind her ears and turned to the younger girl. She felt embarrassed.

'That's all in the past. Let's forget it.' As she said it, she knew that neither of them could.

Over a year after she and Jake had parted, long after Robert's death, she and Tess had bumped into each other in town. Tess had snubbed her with obvious and deliberate anger.

Hurt at such hostility when they had been such friends, Deborah had caught up with her and demanded to know what was wrong.

Tess had been very forthright and Deborah remembered every word.

'Are you trying to tell me that you really don't know?' Tess had said coldly. And when Deborah had protested, she had continued, 'Look, I don't want anything to do with you. I can't forgive you for what you've done to Jake. You're a cold two-timing bitch!'

'What *I've* done to Jake?' Deborah had echoed, but she had been talking to herself. Tess had already walked away.

It had hurt at lot at the time. Tess had obviously not known about Jake's affair with Leila. Perhaps that had been good thing, she idolised Jake after all, fiercely loyal to him. There was no reason why she should be hurt as well.

'Oh, Deborah, I can't forget it,' Tess said now. 'I felt *awful* about it afterwards. I meant to ring you—but somehow I never plucked up the courage.'

Deborah took Tess's hand. 'I understand how you must have felt. You were only sticking up for Jake.'

'It was awful after you left,' Tess burst out, her eyes shadowed. 'Jake started drinking heavily. He was hell to live with, so angry all the time—we all kept out of his way. Then I heard that you'd got married, and I thought, well, you know.'

'Yes, I do know. Please, let's forget it and start again. I always wanted us to stay friends,' Deborah said quickly, unable to explain her feelings or the situation fully. She held out her arms and the two girls embraced.

'Let's go down and join the party,' Deborah said, laughing. 'Everyone will be wondering where you are.'

She checked her face again, so glad that everything was back to normal with Tess. 'Oh,' she remembered, rummaging in her handbag. 'I've bought you a present. Happy birthday.' She watched as Tess tore the paper off the long flat package.

'Oh, Deborah, it's beautiful!' Tess gasped, pulling the bracelet from the satin-lined box. 'I'll wear it now, it goes with my necklace perfectly. Thank you so much.'

As they walked downstairs together, Deborah was going over in her mind what Tess had said about Jake. She found it very hard to believe that he had ever cared enough to turn to drink. Unless—an uncharacteristically cynical smile touched her lips—unless it was just that he couldn't bear to lose.

Music and chatter spilled out of all the rooms

downstairs. Tess was waylaid almost immediately by a tall handsome young man in a white dinner jacket, and whisked away to dance.

Deborah grabbed a glass of champagne from a passing waiter, and wandered towards the room where the band was playing, in search of Oliver.

It was a large high room, crowded with people. Along one wall, linen covered tables groaned under the weight of food, the centre-piece a huge white birthday cake. As she lingered a little uncertainly near the door, a hand touched her shoulder and she nearly jumped out of her skin. Turning, she saw it was Daisy, Jake's housekeeper.

'Miss Deborah, I thought it was you. How nice to see you again.' Daisy had been housekeeper for Jake's grandfather. She was very old-fashioned in her ways and nobody knew how old she was. She seemed perpetually stuck in her fifties, a small rounded women with a tight knot of grey hair above her lined face. The family were often in fear of her, especially Tess. She was strict, with a sharp tongue but she had always been kind to Deborah, and she was smiling now.

'How are you?' Deborah asked, smiling back.

'I'm getting along,' the housekeeper replied with a faintly martyred air.

'It's a lovely party.' Deborah looked around, and her heart suddenly stopped beating. A few feet away stood Jake, his back to her as he chatted to the knot of people gathered around him.

'More work than pleasure for some of us,' Daisy grumbled on. 'You'll excuse me, dear, I can't stand here talking. I have to check the food. You can't trust these catering companies although, of course, Mr Jake got the very best . . .'

Deborah nodded, hardly listening as the housekeeper bustled importantly away.

She was staring at Jake. He was taller than most of the men in the room, his black hair gleaming in the light. He had not seen her yet, so she could watch him undetected, unable to drag her eyes away. The rest of the room disappeared.

He wore a black dinner jacket, superbly tailored to his wide shoulders. The group around him were attentive, respectful, trying to impress him, as people always did. She couldn't see his face, but she could imagine his expression, the grey eyes amused, his mouth straight. He was used to this sort of treatment. He was a man who commanded respect. He wore his strength and power easily.

Deborah watched, hating herself but unable to stop, as a woman joined the group around Jake. A tall slender woman with rich chestnut hair that fell about her face and shoulders in studied disarray. She was very pretty, with sharp vivacious features and sparkling brown eyes. Her dress was buttercup satin, sexy and expensive, and she slid her arm through Jake's with confidence, smiling up into his face, as though she knew her attention was wanted.

Deborah turned away then, a sharp pain stabbing at her inside. Jake's latest lover? she wondered, not examining the pain too closely. What did it matter to her? She didn't want him, did she? Somehow none of her thoughts rang true.

Oliver appeared at her side. 'How about some food? I don't know about you, but I'm starving,' he admitted with a smile.

Deborah could not have eaten a thing, but she allowed him to steer her towards the laden tables, praying that Jake wouldn't see her. As she halfheartedly nibbled on a small piece of Brie, Oliver said, 'He's here, I see.' His voice was casual but he was watching her carefully.

'Yes.' She threw the cheese away, suddenly hating the taste of it.

'Not as bad as you thought?'

'It doesn't bother me at all,' she said airily, but she was lying through her teeth, trying to hide the cracks. 'How was it with Beatrice?' she asked, changing the subject.

Oliver shrugged, not meeting her eyes. 'I don't want to talk about it.'

'Okay.' She immediately wished she hadn't mentioned Beatrice's name.

Tess's voice came over her shoulder. 'Secrets, Oliver?'

Oliver smiled warmly, his mask firmly back in place. 'It all adds to my air of mysterious charm,' he said flippantly, and Tess giggled. Deborah turned smiling, but the smile died on her lips. Around Tess's waist lay Jake's arm. He was standing with his sister and he was only a few inches away from Deborah.

As she looked at him, she realised that some of her horror must be showing on her face, because he was smiling slightly, his eyes cool as they held hers.

She looked away, cursing the colour that was flushing her cheeks. She felt Oliver moving a little closer to her, and knew that he had seen her reaction to Jake. She wanted to act normally, but she couldn't think of a single thing to say.

Luckily Oliver did it for her. 'Great party,' she heard him say.

'Yes, it is, isn't it.' Tess was looking radiantly happy. 'And guess what, Jake's just given me another present.' She looked up into her brother's face, her love in her eyes. From beneath her lashes, Deborah watched Jake smiling down indulgently at the younger girl. She felt her heart beating faster and closed her eyes, wanting only to get away. But as that was impossible, she forced herself to listen to what Tess was saying. 'Jake's bought the lease of a flat in Kensington—isn't it fantastic? I can move in whenever I like. A flat of my own—I can't believe it!'

'That's wonderful.' Deborah carefully avoided looking at Jake, although she was so aware of him that she was trembling.

'Jake's wonderful,' Tess corrected, her eyes shining with excitement.

'I doubt Deborah would agree,' Jake said sardonically, staring at Deborah's downturned face.

'I . . . I don't know what you mean,' she muttered, glaring at him. He smiled. 'Dance with me then,' he suggested smoothly.

With Tess looking on, obviously unaware of the tension between them, there was nothing she could do.

In furious silence she allowed him to lead her on to the dance floor, where as if by order, the fates working against her, the music changed to a slow lilting waltz. She went into his arms stiffly, her heart pounding as he held her.

'Did you arrange this?' she demanded under her breath, taking her anger with herself out on him.

He laughed. 'What do you think?'

'It wouldn't surprise me one little bit.' A tremor ran through her as his hand brushed the bare skin of her back. His fingers were long, tanned, very strong and their gentle touch brought the memories flooding back again. She allowed her own hand to move lightly to his shoulder, surprised to feel the tensing of his muscles beneath the expensively-cut cloth of his jacket.

Looking up into his face, their eyes met, holding. His were narrowed, coolly mocking, giving nothing away.

'You dance very well,' she said, because she had to break the silent tension that was building up between them.

Jake smiled. 'So do you.'

Deborah felt herself flushing at something in his voice. Their bodies fitted together perfectly. She knew that, and she knew he was thinking the same. It had always been so. They moved now as one, hardly aware of the music that guided them, and there was something possessive in Jake's touch at her waist, at her spine. For the first time in three long lonely years, she felt herself falling under his spell again.

His closeness made her feel weak. She felt his strength, his potent male sexuality, and despite all her willpower, she felt herself responding.

'Relax,' Jake murmured, and she realised that she was holding herself tightly, her body rigid with concentration.

'I am relaxed,' she protested, keeping her eyes lowered. 'You're holding me too tightly, that's all. Please let me go.'

In answer, Jake's grip tightened in silence, his eyes suddenly as hard as ice. Forced against the hard disturbing length of his body, she felt herself trembling violently. The heavy muscles of his arms were like bands of steel, and although he was not hurting her, she was left in no doubt as to his immense strength, his dominance.

Jake felt the tremors shaking her body, and his fingers gently brushed the bare skin of her spine. Her skin was like warm silk, smooth and yielding. He felt the muscles tautening in his stomach.

He wanted her, God, how he wanted her. Nothing had

changed, she was still in his blood, despite all that had happened, despite all the bitterness and the years that had separated them.

'I can't let you go,' he said harshly. 'You're wasting your breath asking me to.'

'We had an agreement,' Deborah said in a thin shaking voice. 'For Tess's benefit, remember?'

She could feel the coolness of his breath against her hair, the clean male scent of his skin, and a deep craving was running like fire through her veins. She wanted the touch of his mouth on hers again. She wanted his hunger, his possession. Nobody else had touched her, and she finally admitted that she wanted him. She wanted him with a dizzying aching urgency that made her heart ache.

'Sure, I remember.' His eyes were dark as he stared down into her face. Defeated by the familiar mockery she heard in his voice Deborah bent her head to the width of his shoulder.

I love him, she acknowledged painfully. I've been fooling nobody but myself. I've always loved him, in spite of Leila, in spite of everything. She couldn't deny this fever inside her. It was love. Pure simple love. And perhaps that was why she had been so desperate to keep him at a distance. Perhaps she had always known that if she came too close she wouldn't be able to pretend any more.

She still hated him for his affair with Leila, but she loved him too. Maybe it was true that the line between love and hatred was very, very thin.

Against the cloth of his jacket she said quietly, 'Why did you send me flowers?'

She felt him smile. 'Why not? Didn't you like them?' His voice was still edged with mockery and it hurt her. Beneath her cheek, she could hear the deep steady rhythm of his heart, the rise and fall of his chest as he breathed. Her defeat seemed too much to bear.

'They're beautiful,' she replied in a flat toneless voice.

'You're beautiful—so beautiful tonight,' Jake muttered roughly, almost as though the words were dragged from him against his will.

Deborah lifted her head to look into his dark face, and her eyes were suddenly full of tears.

Jake swore softly. 'I didn't intend to see you again,' he said, and his eyes were violent, his voice very bitter.

Deborah froze. 'Let me go,' she demanded, moving restlessly in his arms, her tears changing to anger. 'Let me go, damn you!'

She felt unreasonably hurt by his words, shocked by the ferocity of the pain they inflicted on her. Her emotions were scraped raw by her own painful and humiliating admission that she still loved him.

'Deborah, for God's sake . . .' His voice was low, vibrant with anger.

'Let me go,' she repeated through clenched teeth, tearing herself from his arms and walking very quickly from the dance floor, from the room.

Her old familiarity with the place guided her steps to the large glass conservatory at the back of the house. Thankfully it was dark and empty giving her the solitude she needed. She had only taken two steps inside when she was spun round to face Jake. His hand moved casually, his fingers gripping her wrist, shackling her.

'Leave me alone!' she told him fiercely, struggling to free herself. It was impossible, and his fingers hurt, biting into her flesh, making her wince. She had not heard him behind her. He always moved so silently, with the graceful menace of some huge cat.

'You're not running away again,' he said darkly, holding her still.

Deborah glared at him with wild bitter eyes. 'I'm going home now. I've had enough of this damned pretence.'

Jake smiled lazily, though his eyes were cold and dark. 'Really? You surprise me,' he drawled softly.

'I don't know what you mean.' She was frightened by the quiet menace in his voice, by the punishing grip that shackled her in this deserted conservatory.

'So sweet, so innocent. I could almost believe you— if I didn't know you better.' His contempt flayed her.

'You don't know me at all!' she hit out. 'And if you don't let me go, I'll scream.'

Jake laughed, derision glittering in his eyes. 'You'd better know that I have no intention of letting you go. You belong to me—you always have, you always will. And you can run and hide from that fact all you want, but it won't change a thing.'

Panic made Deborah struggle to get away from him, but his hold tightened, and using his vastly superior strength, he lifted and turned her trapped hand. His eyes held hers in a long hard glance before he bent his black head, his mouth brushing her palm again and again.

Deborah shuddered, her heart pounding as she watched him. The touch of his mouth was setting her blood on fire, filling her with a desire so powerful, it made her gasp.

When Jake finally lifted his head, she quickly veiled her eyes, desperate to hide from him the way she felt, her love and her hate inextricably mixed.

Without releasing her, he reached out, his fingers touching her throat, resting lightly on the hurried pulse that beat beneath her pale skin. She did not move. She knew that her racing heart was giving her away and she needed to defend herself.

'You insult me,' she said quietly. 'And I *hate* you for that.'

Jake's mouth hardened, his eyes becoming curiously blank. 'You insult your own intelligence by denying what you feel. Did Stevens make you feel like this?' And when she turned her head away, he tilted it back, forcing her to meet the icy grey depths of his eyes. 'How was he in bed? Did he satisfy you? You were always so wild, so abandoned.'

Humiliated colour poured into Deborah's face and his words brought an anger so fierce that she flew at him, her nails ready to claw his face. 'You have no right to talk about Robert like that, and you have no right to talk about me,' she hissed. 'How dare you! How *dare* you!'

Jake caught her hands before they reached him, twisting them easily behind her back. 'You'd be surprised what I dare,' he said with a coolly mocking smile. Dredging up all her scattered reserves of courage, Deborah looked him straight in the eye. 'I doubt it,' she retorted evenly. 'There's nothing you could do that would surprise me. You always were a cold-hearted swine.'

'Another challenge, Deborah?' Jake's dark brows lifted.

'Don't touch me.' Her hard-found courage melted away before the soft menace in his voice. 'I couldn't stand it. I hate you.'

Jake pulled her closer, until their bodies were only inches apart. He stared down at her with narrowed eyes. 'Perhaps that would make it perfect,' he said, very softly. 'Hadn't you thought of that?'

'Oh, I'd thought of it,' she managed through numb

lips. 'You get your kicks from hurting people now, do you?'

She knew that she had angered him, that her insult had found its target. His grip tightened painfully, arching her even closer and she could feel the coolness of his breath against her skin.

'Don't make me angry, Deborah, because I think, I just might enjoy hurting you.'

'You've already proved that!' she shot back, trembling. 'I don't need another lesson, thank you.'

His mouth curved upwards. 'Your eyes tell me a different story, my love.' The murmured endearment held mockery. 'I want to know what Stevens taught you. I've waited a long time to find out.'

'Jake, please . . .' She struggled against him, pleading suddenly.

'Oh, no, Deborah.' He lowered his dark head and found her mouth with his own, in a kiss that was deep and savage and punishing.

Deborah fought him, but she was powerless against his sheer strength. Then, suddenly, that didn't matter, because her body was yielding against his, long-denied and hidden emotions flooding through the careful barriers she had erected around her heart. Hadn't she ached for this moment for three long years? Hadn't she longed for the powerful sensual touch of his mouth?

She stopped struggling, her lips parting beneath the pressure of his. Jake felt her softness, her response and his mouth became gentle. He brushed her parted lips again with an aching tenderness, until she moaned, her arms coming up around his neck, her fingers tangling in his black hair to pull down his head.

The kiss deepened, raw need flaring between them, out of control. Jake's powerful arms held her arching body tightly, his hands slowly caressing her bare spine.

'Oh God,' he muttered into her throat, his breath coming unevenly. Their mouths fused in desperate passion, and Deborah was drowning, her body aching with desire.

Approaching footsteps on the old stones broke them apart. In the quiet conservatory, their glances held, locking. Deborah stared into the dark liquid depths of Jake's eyes and saw his hunger. She didn't even know where she was for a moment. Nothing else mattered except being here with him in this moment in time. She wanted him with a burning urgency that she had never known before and in his face, she saw that his own need equalled hers.

Leila's voice fell into the heavy silence. 'Jake, darling, I've been looking for you everywhere.' She moved towards them. 'And Deborah—Stevens. What a surprise.' She didn't bother to hide her malice.

The spell was broken, and Deborah felt as though she had been doused from head to foot in cold water.

She had forgotten all about Leila. In Jake's arms she had forgotten everything. Leila stood framed in the light from the doorway, dark and beautiful in red satin, her long legs bare. Deborah hadn't even known she was at the party.

'Excuse me.' Without even looking at Jake, she began to walk away. Terrible pain lanced through her as she realised what she had done. How could she have let him kiss her like that? How could she have forgotten Leila. His mistress . . .

With a pale, determined face, she found Oliver. 'I want to leave,' she told him, in a flat expressionless voice. 'I want to leave now.'

CHAPTER SIX

SHE couldn't sleep at all that night. She paced around the flat, her mind running round in circles, a core of aching desire still pulsing inside her.

Why had she gone to the party? Why? It might have saved her pride but that was no comfort to her now.

She could have made some excuse. She could have stayed in Corfu as planned, met Tess at some later date. She could have avoided that party so easily, and avoided meeting Jake again.

She traced the bruised line of her lips with her fingers, her heart constricting with pain. Oh God, she wanted him so much. She had been running for so long, she had forgotten that she would never stop loving him. It was the kind of love that came once in a lifetime, the kind of love that would never fade.

She made some coffee and forced herself to sit down. Questions plagued her. Was he still having an affair with Leila? Who was the woman in the yellow dress? From her own bitter experience she knew that one woman could not satisfy him. From what Tess had said, she knew how her own behaviour must have looked at the time of their parting. He assumed that she had been seeing Robert all the time. The fact that she and Robert had been married must have confirmed his suspicions. It served him right, she thought spitefully. He could think what he liked. She had no intention of seeing him again. Tonight had been a mistake she had no intention of repeating.

She finally fell asleep on the couch as dawn was

breaking and she woke two hours later feeling terrible. The thought of driving up to Kendal filled her with unusual dismay. Cole had made the appointment for her as soon as he knew she was back from holiday, and there was no getting out of it. She had found refuge in her work before. Perhaps she could find it again.

Struggling up from the couch, massaging her aching muscles, she switched on the percolator before taking a hot shower. The water splashed over her, easing her tiredness, and she wondered for the millionth time how she could love a man who had been so flagrantly unfaithful to her. She halted her thoughts, not wanting to think about him and yet unable to stop.

She dressed while she drank her coffee, choosing a black, button-through, cashmere dress with a matching gaberdine coat and soft leather boots. It was chic and fashionable and very businesslike, which was what Cole expected when she was representing the company. She pulled her hair back into a neat chignon and made up her face, carefully hiding the tell-tale dark circles beneath her eyes.

Ready on time, she collected her briefcase, portfolio and handbag and left the flat. Oliver was in the hall as she went down, pulling the newspaper from the letterbox. 'You're early,' he remarked with a smile.

'I'm going to Kendal—remember? I told you last night.'

'Did you? I'm more interested in what you didn't tell me.' He shot her a long hard look and she knew he could see right through her careful make-up.

'What are you talking about?'

'Jake Logan,' Oliver said succinctly. 'It's far too early in the morning for games, dear stepsister.'

'I haven't got time.'

'Look, I left a perfectly good party just as it was

hotting up, to drive you home—so I think you owe me an explanation.' His smile was sweet, softening his words.

'I'll tell you later,' she promised, knowing he was only concerned about her. 'But I really must go now. I don't want to be late, Cole would kill me.'

'The forecast is snow up north,' Oliver said, scanning the newspaper. Deborah didn't really care.

'Well, if I have to stay over, Cole will be footing the hotel bill. See you later.'

In the car she switched on the radio, but the music and bright chatter frayed her nerves, so she switched it off again and concentrated on her driving.

The motorway was fairly clear from the Midlands onwards, though the sky was heavy with snow. She arrived in Kendal with an hour to spare so she had coffee in a tiny tea house she found on the main road through the town.

Cole's prospective client lived in an enormous architect-designed house a few miles out of Kendal, and she drove through the gates with ten minutes to spare. The meeting went well, though it took all afternoon. Cole believed in the personal touch and because his time was so short, Deborah had gradually become one of his top sales executives, as well as a designer. She was beautiful and well groomed, and she knew what she was talking about, Cole had told her. She was the perfect advertisement for the company. It was true that being one of the designers she knew the business inside out. It was a challenge that she enjoyed, though these sales trips were comparatively rare.

The company, though based in Los Angeles, was breaking into the British market, and all prospective clients were given a personal visit. Cole would have come himself if he hadn't been tied up in meetings with the chairman of a chain of London shops.

The client, Mr Ainley, owned a number of exclusive boutiques in the North of England, and was interested in new lines. So, with the ground work completed and Mr Ainley very definitely interested, Deborah left his house a little after five o'clock. At the gates she pulled to a halt, undecided as to what she would do. The sky was dark and it was snowing, and she knew that if she wanted to get home tonight, she ought to be heading towards the motorway.

A sudden loneliness gripped her. Inside the warm cocoon of the car she was safe from the weather but cut off from the world. She thought of Jake, his hard face rising up in her mind's eye, and felt like crying. She was tired of being alone, she was tired of being unloved. At this moment she wanted someone to lean on, someone to talk to. She wanted the strength of a man's arms around her. She couldn't fool herself. She wanted Jake. More than anyone in the world, more than anyone in her life, she wanted Jake.

Slamming the car into gear, she turned out of the drive, the tyres squealing. She was angry with herself for being all kinds of a fool. Jake had never loved her, he never would. If she wasn't careful, she would spend the rest of her life longing for him, loving him so much she would never be able to look at another man. It was a depressing prospect.

Reaching the motorway, she stopped the car. The snow was heavier now and she wasn't sure whether to drive on. She could drive back to Kendal and spend the night in a hotel. She didn't feel like driving back to London.

She lit a cigarette, and swallowed back the tears that were suddenly blurring her vision. You're an idiot, she told herself, such an idiot. Then, on impulse, she turned the car around, and joined the motorway on the other carriageway, driving north towards the Lakes. By the time she reached Windermere, visibility was down to a few feet and she was forced to crawl along at ten miles an hour. She didn't examine her motives, but she knew exactly where she was going.

It took her an hour to reach the cottage, even though it was only a few miles from the town. The car was skidding badly, the tyres not gripping the icy road and she would have been frightened to death if she hadn't been so determined to reach her destination. In the end she had to leave it and walk the final quarter of a mile. By the time she reached the front door, she was soaked through, the snow driven into her face by a bitter wind. From the high white drifts, it was clear that heavy snow had fallen over the past few days, and the temperature was very much lower than in London.

The key was where it always was, under a plant pot near the door, and she knew that Charlotte would not mind her using the cottage. As she opened the door, piles of snow fell inside. She scooped it out with her hands, a feeling of profound relief coming over her as the door shut behind her.

The cottage smelled damp and unused and she stumbled in the darkness searching for the light switch. Finding it, she pulled the switch and nothing happened. She tried again. Nothing. Cursing, she fumbled in her handbag and found her lighter.

She tried every switch she could find with the same result. There was no electricity. The fuse box offered no answers. None of the fuses were blown and the mains switch was turned on. She shivered. She shouldn't have come here. The cottage was hardly used in the winter and it would be impossible to stay the night in any comfort.

She walked over to the front door, intending to drive back to Kendal. A blizzard of snow whirled in on her, her footprints already hidden. She was going nowhere.

Trying to make the best of it, she lit a fire from the neat pile of logs in the fireplace. She found a decanter of brandy and some candles in the carved oak sideboard. The spirit warmed her, and made her realise how tired she was, sudden waves of exhaustion washing over her. She lay down on the sofa, her coat draped over her, and stared into the fire, her eyelids drooping. It isn't so bad after all, she thought with a smile. I'll get up in a minute and throw more logs on the fire. I could freeze to death if it goes out . . .

She woke with a start, two hours later, sure that something had woken her. She was cold and the darkness frightened her, as she lay, ears straining against the silence. The fire had gone out, the room chilled again.

She heard footsteps outside the front door, footsteps muffled in the snow. She swallowed, unable to move, her heart pounding loudly in her ears. There was someone outside.

She couldn't see, but she could hear the slight creaking of the door handle being turned. Had she locked it? She couldn't remember. She must have done because the door didn't open and she let out her breath on a long high-pitched sigh.

She sat up, trying to pull herself together. She didn't want to be lying on the couch if there was an intruder outside. She felt vulnerable, weak and nervous, and she nearly jumped out of her skin when she heard the banging on the door.

'Who is it?' she shouted shakily.

'Jake, let me in.'

Laughing with relief she ran to the door and opened it. He stood outside, tall and powerful in the darkness. She wasn't surprised to see him. It was as if she had known he would come.

'You frightened me,' she admitted, still smiling.

'Let me in,' he repeated, his eyes holding hers, unsmiling. Hard.

She stood back and he brushed past her as he came inside. His hair was wet, his coat heavy with snow, the cold dark smell of the night clung to him. Deborah closed the door and turned to him. She felt his anger as he spoke. 'Why the hell are you in the dark?'

'There's no power,' she said, her voice breathless.

He seemed to fill the room with his presence and she felt intimidated.

'I've found some candles, though.' She moved carefully across the room, finding her lighter by touch. She lit two yellow candles, their ghostly flickering bringing the room to life. She picked one up, holding it high, and because her hands were shaking, burning wax spilled on to her fingers. She cried out involuntarily, and Jake was beside her in a second.

'You stupid little bitch,' he muttered, taking the candle from her and examining her burnt fingers. His sure touch made her tremble.

She looked into his hard face. 'Don't——' she began, but he cut her off.

'What are you doing here, anyway? You could have got yourself killed.'

'I don't know why I'm here,' she said defiantly. 'Why are you?'

Jake released her hand but did not move away. 'I followed you.'

'How did you know . . .?'

'I rang your office. Your secretary was very helpful.' His mouth curved into a slow smile, and Deborah felt a flash of anger. She could just imagine him charming Alison, winding her round his little finger to get the information he wanted.

'That information was *supposed* to be confidential,' she said stiffly.

Jake laughed. 'Your secretary can't keep a secret then.'

'How did you know I'd come to the cottage?' She diverted the conversation from Alison because she could feel that old bitter jealousy rising to the surface.

'I guessed you'd come here,' Jake said calmly.

She turned away, hiding her eyes from him. 'How predictable I must be.'

He reached out and caught her chin in his fingers, forcing her to meet his eyes. He scrutinised her face, seeing the tears barely held back, the sudden pain.

'No,' he said very softly. 'Not predictable. Never predictable.'

'I'm going back to Kendal,' she said through clenched teeth, sure he was laughing at her. 'Now.'

Jake smiled, but his eyes were very cool. 'Don't be ridiculous. You're going nowhere.'

'You can't hold me against my will,' she snapped, pulling away from him, aware that she was being melodramatic.

Jake lit a cigarette, drawing on it deeply, the fragrant smoke drifting from his nostrils. 'Your car is completely buried,' he said, expressionlessly. 'It would take you hours to dig it out, even if the roads were passable.'

'You could take me in your car.'

'The situation is the same,' he said patiently.

'But there's not enough room here for both of us,' Deborah said desperately, the thought of having to spend the night with him in this dark isolated cottage filling her with panic. 'You can go to your own house—it's not far from here.'

Jake frowned, his voice irritated now. 'The roads are closed, for God's sake. If you don't believe me, go out and look for yourself. My car is in a ditch half a mile from here, so stop acting like a child and accept the fact that we are both staying here tonight.'

He shrugged out of his coat with easy grace, and Deborah, swaying with tiredness, watched dry-mouthed. 'Sit down,' Jake instructed curtly. 'You look like death.'

'Thank you!' Huddled on the couch, shivering, she reflected that she didn't need him to tell her that.

'What about the bed upstairs?' His voice was cool and businesslike but Deborah felt the colour pouring into her face.

'It's cold and damp. It needs airing,' she said shortly, the tilt of her head defiant.

Jake nodded, smiling slightly, and while she sat, her limbs slack with exhaustion, he collected blankets, relit the fire and opened some tins of meat and fish found in the pantry. They ate in silence, washing the food down with brandy. Deborah stared into the flames of the fire, warm now, and strangely content. On the mantelpiece, the candles flickered, their soft glow throwing a cocoon of intimacy across the room.

Out of the corner of her eyes, she watched Jake smoking, aware of every slight shifting of his long powerful body. She tried, but she couldn't drag her eyes away. Whenever she was with him she couldn't stop looking at him, her fascination deep and soul-destroying.

He turned his black head and their eyes met.

'Why did you come here?' he asked again.

'I told you, I don't know.' She looked away, breaking the eye contact. It was true. She really didn't know. Her feelings for him and for this place were so deep, so complicated that she didn't dare to reach down and inspect them. The knowledge that she had never stopped loving him, that she never would, had been enough of a shock, she was still getting over it.

'Think about it,' Jake suggested mockingly.

Deborah leaned back, closing her eyes. 'Too many questions,' she murmured, smiling lazily.

'I've got plenty more.' He moved quickly and silently.

She heard the threat in his voice and her eyes flew open. He was standing over her. The warm contentment fled, the room suddenly full of savage electric tension.

'Jake——' Frightened, she gazed up into his unreadable face.

'Tell me about Robert Stevens,' he demanded grimly.

'No, I won't.' She stood up, feeling too vulnerable with him towering over her. But as she tried to move away he caught her shoulders, his fingers biting into her flesh as he turned her to face him. 'I want to know,' he said angrily, shaking her slightly.

'It's none of your damned business,' she retorted, hating him for his strength, unable to understand his obsession with a dead man.

'You were seeing him behind my back. I'd say that made it my business, wouldn't you?' His eyes were hot, burning with rage. 'God knows, I could kill you for what you did.'

'It didn't bother you for three years,' Deborah said

bitterly, twisting her body in an effort to free herself. 'So why now?'

'You married him,' Jake said through his teeth. 'You were his wife.'

'I wouldn't have thought a little formality like that would bother *you*!' She spat at him, her voice shaking. 'I read the newspapers, I know what sort of a man you are.'

She had gone too far, driven by the fierce emotions he aroused in her. Jake's hands were violent, but as his mouth found hers, she couldn't pretend that she didn't want it.

She had been thinking about him, aching for his touch since their parting the night before. His mouth explored hers deeply, his anger dissolving in desperate need. Heat flamed between them, hunger in the fusing of their mouths. Deborah moaned softly. He had taught her body the motions of desire, of love. He had taught her so well, and she longed to experience his lovemaking again. Her fingers traced the tensed muscles of his shoulders, sliding beneath the fine material of his shirt to find his hair-roughened chest. She touched him, caressed him, as she had dreamed of doing so often. His skin was smooth and tanned, so familiar, the fine abrasive texture of the hair that matted his chest, well remembered.

Jake shuddered, lifting his mouth from hers, brushing her lips gently. 'God, Deborah, you're driving me insane,' he muttered, his breath coming unevenly. He stilled her seeking hands, covering them with his own. He stared down into her face with dark, narrowed eyes. 'How many times did you go to him, straight from me?' he asked, harshly. 'How many?'

Deborah stiffened, afraid that she had given too much away in those wild desperate moments in his arms. She couldn't bear him to know that she loved him. Had he been testing her, in some perverse way? Did he already know?

'Does it matter?' she asked, defensively.

'Dammit, yes!' His anger scraped along her nerves.

'Well, I don't know,' she lied, unable to shed her pride and tell him the truth. 'I don't know.'

Jake's mouth hardened. He looked as though he was going to hit her, fighting for, and finally gaining control of his anger.

'Why?' The one word question was torn from him, his mouth twisting bitterly. Deborah bit her lip, her lashes sweeping down to hide her eyes. 'I won't talk about Robert, I won't. You're not so blameless yourself.'

'Meaning?' His voice was ominous. He was very still, reminding her of a dark panther, poised for the kill.

'I'm too tired to fight,' she pleaded, something inside her breaking. She couldn't mention Leila, she was sick of arguing, close to tears, shaking. Jake looked at her, taking in the paleness of her face, the dark smudges beneath her eyes.

'Go to sleep then,' he said quietly, surprising her. 'You can have the couch. We'll talk tomorrow.'

'Thank you.' She tried to make her voice sound light and sarcastic, but failed miserably. She fled from the room feeling foolish.

In the kitchen, she washed in freezing cold water, staring out of the window. Outside the sky was clear. Amazingly, the snow had stopped falling, and the heavy blanketed silence rang in her ears.

She ran back to the fire, shivering, holding out her hands to warm them. She felt embarrassed as she unzipped her boots, but glancing surreptitiously at

Jake, she found his face impassive. He wasn't even looking at her. She lay down awkwardly, visibly jumping as he moved towards her.

'Relax.' He had seen her reaction, and a lazy amused mockery threaded his voice. 'You're perfectly safe with me, so don't overestimate your attractions.'

'You wanted me before,' Deborah heard herself reminding him, her voice quivering with rejection.

'Is that an invitation, my love?' His eyes were very dark, his mouth sensual, as he stared down at her.

'Go to hell!' She buried her face against her arms, hearing his soft laughter with her teeth grinding together.

Damn him, she thought furiously. He was too strong, too sure of himself, and he always won. She felt him covering her with blankets and did not move. She closed her eyes and willed herself to go to sleep. She seemed to dream for hours, dreams filled with anxiety and dread. In them, she was running, pursued by a dark, faceless figure. She couldn't get away, her legs leaden, refusing to carry her.

She woke with a scream, Jake's name on her lips. He was beside her in a moment, taking the hand she held out to him, engulfing it in his own.

'You've been dreaming,' he said quietly.

'Oh.' She lay back with relief. Her forehead was damp with perspiration. 'It was horrible.' She shuddered, remembering.

'You're safe now.' Jake's eyes were smiling, his long fingers moving against her palm.

Deborah nodded, turning her face away, embarrassed by the tenderness of the mood between them.

'You look like a little girl when you're asleep,' he said, staring at her averted profile.

Her head swung round in shock. He had been

watching her sleeping. She felt vulnerable, disturbed by the knowledge. She looked into his dark grey eyes and her stomach lurched.

'Who was that woman at the party?' she asked in a small voice.

'What woman?' His smile was indulgent.

'The one in the yellow dress.' She didn't know what had brought it into her mind. A truthful answer would probably hurt her, and of course it was none of her business.

'Ah, that was Caroline. Caroline Winters.' He said it as though he was amused by her question.

The name rang a bell immediately. Caroline Winters had been in Jake's car at the time of the accident. 'Is she your lover?' Her own brazen courage amazed her.

Their eyes met, and tension filled the room, dizzying in its intensity. Jake frowned heavily. 'Don't judge everybody by your own standards.'

It was as though he had hit her. For a second she couldn't breathe. 'My standards?' she echoed bitterly, her anger exploding. 'Damn you, Jake Logan, damn you to hell!'

His mouth tightened, and he reached out, his fingers twisting in the pale gold of her hair. 'Damn me by all means, but I'll take you with me,' he promised, very softly.

'Don't touch me,' she whispered, trembling as his fingers moved against her head. 'I hate it.'

Jake laughed, a harsh humourless sound, his hands straying to her white throat, caressing with strange gentleness. Deborah gasped, frightened, suddenly aware of how alone they were cut off from the world in this tiny isolated cottage.

She looked into the smoky, unsmiling depths of his

eyes and accepted that this was exactly where she wanted to be. She had come here, somehow knowing that he would come too. It had almost been an invitation.

'You followed me,' she said, smiling, the curve of her lips unknowingly provocative.

'Yes.' Jake's voice was husky, liquid.

'Why?'

'You know why. No games, Deborah.' His fingers moved against her throat and he watched her with narrowed eyes. Deborah bent her head, his gentle touch aching along every nerve in her body. 'No,' she said on a sigh. It was a denial of everything that was happening, everything that had gone before. 'Jake, please . . .'

He tilted up her face, staring into her eyes. 'Don't lie to yourself, Deborah, don't lie to me.' His voice was hard. 'You came here for the same reason I did. It's not over between us. It never will be. I want you with a hunger that tears away at me twenty-four hours a day, a hunger I can't feed with anyone else.'

Deborah's heart lurched violently. She gazed at him, her mouth dry. He was describing her own feelings exactly. Jake read the expression in her wide shocked eyes. 'It's the same for you,' he said quietly.

'I don't want it to be that way,' she whispered in anguish. 'It frightens me.' He was talking about desire. He would never talk about love.

'God, do you think I do?' The bitter anger in his voice jerked her head up. His eyes were burning with emotion, his shoulders hunched with tension. She swallowed with difficulty. 'What about Leila?'

'What about her?' He sounded impatient, as though the question was irrelevant.

'Is she . . . is she your lover?' She knew she was provoking an explosion, but she had to ask.

'Dammit, no!' Jake muttered through clenched teeth, as though pushed beyond endurance. His fury filled the room, as he swore violently. 'Do you think I sleep with every women I came into contact with?'

Deborah flinched. 'How should I know? It certainly wouldn't surprise me.' She felt raw, hurt, her heart squeezing with pain. She needed some defence against him and the feelings he could arouse so effortlessly. She needed to believe that he was lying, but defeated, she couldn't. She was attacking him because it was the only form of defence she had. And it didn't seem to be working.

'You little bitch,' he said, breathing quickly.

'At least Robert married me,' she threw at him desperately, as though the words were a talisman of protection, her courage failing by the second.

Jake froze, his eyes darkening to black, his mouth cruel. 'God, I could kill you for that,' he said hoarsely. A shiver of fear ran down Deborah's spine. She moved away a little, regretting her own rash words, knowing that it was far too late to back away.

'I'm bored with talking,' she said, with all the coolness she could muster. 'I want to get some sleep.' She flashed him a pointed glance. 'Do you mind?'

Jake was silent for a moment, his face a cold, expressionless mask. Then he smiled, a slow cruel smile, that left Deborah shaking inside.

'Oh yes, I mind,' he said too softly. 'I haven't finished with you yet.'

Deborah couldn't speak, her face paling as she read his dark expression.

'No, Jake . . .' she said, her voice shaking violently. 'No . . .'

He laughed, holding her glance, a naked desire flaring in his eyes, as he looked at her, a desire so powerful that she was hypnotised with fear. It stripped away everything but his need, and she felt an unbidden response aching into life inside herself. His eyes were glittering, his face taut, the bones hard. His strength terrified her. His strength, his desire, and his anger. She watched, unable to move a muscle as his hands reached out slowly.

'Don't . . .' she whispered, as he pulled the pins from her hair, so that it fell loose about her shoulders.

He looked at her, his face all shadowed angles in the candlelight, his eyes black, glinting.

'It's as though we've never been apart,' he said quietly, threading his fingers through the loosened silk of her hair, feeling the texture, the shining thickness against her skin. 'Three years is a hell of a long time to wait.'

Holding herself rigid, Deborah abandoned her pride and whispered. 'Please, Jake, let me go.'

He shook his head. 'I can't,' he said thickly. 'I have to know what Stevens taught you.'

He bent, his mouth against her throat, kissing her skin tenderly, unhurriedly. She shuddered at his touch, desire racing through her body, heating her blood. She wanted to push him away, but she couldn't move, couldn't protest.

Jake raised his head, staring into her eyes, as his hands began unbuttoning the cashmere dress. She felt the sensual brush of his fingers against her bare skin, moving lower, until the dress fell away altogether.

'Jake——' The words wouldn't come and she knew that he saw the fever in her eyes. Taking her body between his hands, his mouth parted hers in a deep savage kiss that made her head spin. She couldn't control her response. It was as hot as fire and as violent as his demand.

He didn't offer tenderness now, only desire and as his mouth plundered hers, Deborah felt her control slipping away. She didn't want to feel like this. If she let him make love to her now, she would hate herself, despise her own weakness. But she felt Jake's mouth kissing her naked breasts, and moaned, arching back her head, her inhibitions dissolving. She wanted him, so badly. She couldn't fight the sensations that were running through her like a tidal wave.

Then suddenly, she was past coherent thought, reaching for him blindly. He shuddered as she touched him, his mouth finding hers again, lifting her into his powerful arms and laying her gently on the rug in front of the fire. His burning glance swept slowly over her nakedness, his hands exploring the soft familiar curves of her body.

It was a deliberate act of possession. He touched her with a lingering slowness, easing the long-unsatisfied need inside himself. He stared down at her pale slender body, his breath coming quickly and unevenly. He kissed her flesh, following the path laid bare by his hands. He made love to her slowly, holding back, reining his own desire as he aroused her, until Deborah reached for him, pulling him down, her hands touching his smooth powerful shoulders, his deep chest, crying out his name as he entered her.

His mouth bruised hers with a devouring intensity, the trust of his body betraying his agonising need.

She clung to him, shaking, no longer aware of anything but his strength, his mastery and the desire that was almost too fierce to bear. She knew that she cried out her love for him. She couldn't help herself.

She held him, her nails raking his smooth skin, her body yielding, opening beneath his, and for the first time in three long, empty years, Jake possessed what had always been his.

She gave him everything, her body, her soul, forgetting in her abandonment that it had never been enough, that in the cold light of day there would be nothing but regrets.

CHAPTER SEVEN

FIVE weeks later, Deborah realised that she was pregnant.

She woke one morning with a feeling of nausea in her stomach. She climbed out of bed, wondering if it could be something she had eaten at dinner with Cole, the night before.

In the kitchen she spooned coffee into the percolator and switched it on, and as the fragrant smell of the beans filled the room, she knew she was going to be sick. She staggered dizzily into the bathroom and vomited into the basin.

She seemed to lean for ages against the cool tiles, retching violently, but the sickness and dizzyness finally subsided and she splashed her face with cold water.

Back in the kitchen, she switched off the percolator, unable to face the thought of coffee and mentally went through what she had eaten the night before.

She and Cole had dined late, after a particularly long day at the office. Deborah had chosen cold duck and salad, followed by fresh raspery tart. She hadn't eaten much at all, her appetite was small these days. Surely it couldn't have been . . .?

Her eyes lighted on the calender and the glass of water she had been sipping fell from her fingers, smashing on the tiled floor. She looked at the date, and for a moment she couldn't breathe. Two weeks overdue. She hadn't even noticed. She had been so caught up with avoiding Jake, with concentrating on her work . . .

Defeated, she rested her head in her hands, the full implications of the situation sinking in, and burst into tears. She didn't hear Oliver entering the flat.

He strolled into the kitchen whistling. 'I did knock . . .' he began cheerfully, then, 'Deborah, what on earth's the matter?'

He looked around the kitchen at the shattered glass on the floor, at Deborah, deathly pale and crying her eyes out. 'What is it?' he demanded again, when she didn't answer.

Deborah made an effort to pull herself together. 'I think I'm pregnant,' she blurted out, and immediately wished she hadn't.

Oliver looked surprised, but his voice was casual as he asked. 'Are you sure? Have you seen a doctor?'

'No, I only—no.' She hadn't even thought of it. She would have to have a test. It might be a false alarm, after all, she hadn't been eating or sleeping properly. It could be that she was run down, or anaemic. She could be jumping to conclusions.

'I'm scared,' she admitted, folding her arms across her breasts, hugging herself.

'It'll be okay,' Oliver smiled, and bent to kiss her forehead. 'Go and wash your face, and I'll make some tea.'

Deborah did as she was told, numbly staring at her red eyes in the bathroom mirror. She looked a positive sight, and even the cold water did nothing to help. She touched the flatness of her stomach with her fingers. Was she really carrying Jake's child? Hysterical laughter rose in her throat. It couldn't be true. It just *couldn't*!

She had not seen him since that night at the cottage.

With a sense of desolation, she remembered waking in the darkness, lying still in his arms, her hair against his naked shoulders, his throat. She had felt drained, utterly miserable. Beneath her cheek, she had felt the deep strong rhythm of his heart. She lay still for an hour, his powerful arms holding her tightly, his hand curved over her breast, possessively. It had been the worst kind of agony to leave, but she would have been unable to face him in the cold clear light of the morning.

So she had crept about in the dark, hardly daring to breathe, dressing, collecting her things. She had left without waking him.

Luckily, it had not been snowing and with the help of a passing farmer and his tractor, she had finally managed to get her car back on to the main road.

Back in London she had been staying with a friend. Running away, hiding, she thought with self-contempt. Jake had been trying to get in touch with her. He had telephoned a number of times. He had been to the flat. He had been angry, Oliver had told her that, angry because he knew she was deliberately avoiding him.

Two weeks ago he had stopped telephoning. She had heard from Tess that he was in France on business, so she had come back to the flat. She felt so foolish, so weak. She knew that in the end she would have to face him. After that night in the cottage, they would have to see each other again, but she still didn't feel strong enough to face him. He would know now that she loved him, and that was too humiliating to bear.

She couldn't put him out of her mind for a single second, even though she knew that her love was not reciprocated. He wanted her, as she wanted him. It was an all-consuming explosive desire. She couldn't deny that any more than she could resist it. Knowing, in some deep secret part of her, that he would follow her to Windermere, she had gone there because she needed to see him, because she had needed to experience the soul-destroying satisfaction of his lovemaking one more time.

He was right. It would never be over between them. There would be nobody else for her, not as long as she lived.

She picked up a comb and pulled it through her hair. It was all so hopeless, she felt like crying again, and she longed for the comfort of Jake's arms, for his strength to lean on. And the worst thing was, that if she got in touch with him, she could have that comfort, that strength. He had offered tenderness the night they had been together, albeit after he had forced her to submit without reserve. She didn't understand why, but it had always been that way between them.

It would be so easy to submit, so easy and so pleasurable. A tiny voice of reason forced its way into her consciousness. Jake wanted her now—but how long would it last? Six months? A year, maybe? And that was optimistic. If she allowed their affair to continue, wouldn't she be hurt all over again? And would she have the strength to recover a second time?

She groaned, covering her face with her hands. Was she such a fool that she was longing to make the same mistake again? When she was alone, it was so easy to promise herself that she wouldn't become involved again. When she was with Jake, it was a different story. Her body and her heart turned traitor and she didn't have the strength to fight herself as well as him.

Which was why she would continue keeping out of his way. She would avoid him like the plague.

She let out her breath on a long shaking sigh, fighting the treacherous longing she could feel inside. If she was pregnant—the complications were too enormous to think about. She would have the test before even daring to think about it. There was no point in piling up problems unnecessarily.

Oliver had made a pot of tea and some toast. She sat down at the kitchen table, pale but in control of herself. Oliver poured the tea into two cups. 'Have something to eat,' he said, staring at her.

Deborah looked at the pile of thin toast and felt sick again. 'I couldn't.'

'You should eat something. You're as thin as a rake,' Oliver reproved, frowning.

'I'm not hungry,' she said firmly, sipping the hot tea, enjoying it.

Oliver ate the toast himself, watching her the whole time. 'We'll go and see Ralph. He'll tell you, one way or the other.'

Ralph Taylor was one of Oliver's closest friends, a doctor, with a general practice nearby.

Deborah nodded, grateful that Oliver wasn't asking any questions. 'I suppose it's the best thing.'

'It is.' He stood up. 'Come on, let's go now and get it over with.'

Deborah was a mass of nerves as they drove to the surgery. She wanted it to be a false alarm, but Ralph Taylor, in his quiet pleasant way, confirmed the worst. She was pregnant with Jake's child.

Oliver drove her back to the flat in silence. She felt panic-stricken, not knowing how she would cope, not knowing what to do next. She had the feeling that Oliver was angry, even though he said nothing, and that worried her too.

Back home, he came upstairs with her. 'I'll make some coffee,' he said, his face grim. 'I don't know about you, but I'm dying for a cup.'

'I'm not an invalid, so don't treat me like one,' Deborah snapped, irritated because he was talking to her as though she was a child.

'You don't want a cup of coffee?' He was half smiling, obviously amused by her bad temper.

Deborah smiled too. 'I'm sorry,' she said, knowing that she had been unfair. 'Actually, I'd love one.'

In the kitchen she stood looking out of the window, and felt herself trembling, her eyes filling with tears. 'I don't know what to do,' she said, not turning round.

She felt Oliver's hand touch her shoulder, his voice close, angry. 'It's Logan's, isn't it? Dammit, I thought that was all over, I thought you were finished with him.'

Deborah nodded in silence, and he continued, 'You don't have to have it, you know, not if you don't want to.' She flicked the tears from her cheeks with her fingers, and thought about that, rejecting it immediately, instinctively. She couldn't kill the unborn life inside her. She couldn't kill Jake's child.

'I don't want an abortion,' she replied firmly.

Oliver turned her round to face him. 'You haven't thought about it.'

'I have, I couldn't do it.' She looked at him, and he saw that she meant it.

'You'll have to tell him, then,' he said flatly.

'Why?' The thought filled her with horror.

'Come on.' Oliver lifted his hands in an angry gesture. 'How the hell do you think you can bring up a child with no help, no support?'

'I won't ask him for money,' Deborah said, angry

with herself, because he was asking all the questions she had no answers for. 'It's not his problem.'

'No?' Oliver laughed humourlessly. 'You've got to be realistic, Deborah. He's got a right to know. It's his child as well.'

'I know, I know.' Near to tears again, she sank into a chair and rested her head in her hands. Oliver poured the coffee, and pushed a handkerchief towards her. His voice was gentler as he said, 'Oh, Deb, I'm sorry. I shouldn't be harassing you at a time like this. You should be resting, or whatever it is pregnant women do.'

Deborah managed a shaky smile and sipped her coffee gratefully. 'How would you feel if you found out that Beatrice was pregnant?' she asked curiously.

Oliver's mouth twisted. 'I certainly wouldn't believe it was mine,' he said, then seeing that Deborah was deadly serious. 'Really, I'd be bloody delighted.'

'It was an unfair question.' Deborah hated herself for her tactlessness, her selfishness. 'I'm sorry.'

Oliver shrugged. 'It doesn't matter, honestly it doesn't. Besides, you know damn well that it's irrelevant.'

'Yes.' She couldn't fool Oliver. He knew her too well. 'But I don't think Jake would want to be saddled with a child.'

'You don't know that.' Oliver was being maddeningly reasonable.

'I do.' She heard her voice breaking, giving her away.

'You still love him,' Oliver said flatly. Deborah didn't answer. There was nothing to say.

Oliver left soon after, and she paced the flat, trying to get things into perspective. To find herself pregnant was a shock. It seemed extraordinary that she had conceived so easily during that one night with Jake. But beneath the anxiety and the worry about the future, she felt a tiny, unexpected dart of happiness. If she was honest, she wanted the child. She didn't know why. Her reasons were too deep-rooted, her emotions too mixed up.

Feeling brighter than she had done for weeks, she took a shower, then spent the rest of the day cleaning the flat. Because she had been away, there was a lot of dust and it was a relief to throw herself into some physical work.

She finished at seven, exhausted, glad to put her feet up with a cup of coffee.

Around her, the furniture shone, everything spick and span, the faint smell of lavender polish in the air. She would have a bath, she thought, a long hot bath. Then perhaps she would make an omelette. Something light. She couldn't face the thought of a heavy meal, even though her stomach was empty.

When the doorbell rang, she went to answer it without hesitation, expecting to see Oliver outside, her heart leaping into her throat as she saw Jake leaning indolently against the door jamb. She was instantly aware of what a mess she must look, her hair dragged back, no make-up and dirty old clothes.

'Jake . . .' she said stupidly, still in a state of shock.

'Very observant.' His voice was very cool, his mouth a hard line.

'What do you want?' His coldness sparked off defensive anger and she was sharp with him.

'Let me in and I'll tell you,' he said mockingly, straightening away from the wall, his hands in the pockets of his jeans.

'We have nothing to say to each other,' she protested weakly, overwhelmed by the sight of him. She held the door half closed, blocking his entrance.

'*No?*' The dark grey eyes held hers and an indefinable tension seemed to fill the air. 'Are you going to let me in?'

He stepped forward, towering over her, and with a defeated shrug of her shoulders, she was forced to move back.

In the lounge he turned to her, appraising her slowly from head to toe before his dark glance returned to her face.

'Why have you come?' she asked, trembling. 'What do you want? I thought we'd said everything that needed to be said . . .'

Jake's mouth hardened. 'As I recall, you said nothing. You just ran out on me.'

'It was the only thing to do,' Deborah muttered, embarrassed colour pouring into her face. And when Jake was silent. 'The best thing to do, under the circumstances . . .'

'Best for who?' he countered harshly.

'For both of us.' She bit her lip. 'I didn't know what else . . .'

'Aren't you going to offer me a drink?' He changed the subject abruptly, his eyes still brooding on her flushed face. Deborah frowned. 'I've only got tea or coffee—'

'Coffee will be fine,' he replied politely.

In the kitchen, her hands shook as she got the cups out of the cupboard. Why was he here, she wondered, looking at herself in the tiny mirror on the door, and noticing, with an inward groan, that her face was smeared with dirt. And why did she have to look such a sight?

She smoothed back her hair and washed her face, before making up the tray. Surely he didn't know? There was no way that he could, she thought, her heart pounding. She had only found out herself that morning.

She deliberately took her time, nerves fluttering in her stomach, but in the end she had to go back into the lounge.

Jake was standing at the window, a tall powerful figure in jeans and a dark shirt. He turned as she came in, taking the tray from her shaking hands.

'I can manage,' she protested, on the defensive immediately.

'Can you?' His low voice was openly sceptical. He took in the sleepless shadows beneath her eyes, the lines of tension around her beautiful straight mouth. 'I doubt it, I doubt it very much.'

Deborah bit back an acid retort. She was fully aware that in a battle of wits, she could not win.

They drank the coffee in silence. Glancing at Jake from beneath her lashes, Deborah's heart constricted with anguish. She loved him so much.

She allowed herself to dream for a moment, imagining that he returned her love. How beautifully simple it would be. She would tell him about the baby and he would be happy . . . She dragged her thoughts back to the present, admonishing herself sternly. Foolish dreams like that could only hurt her.

Oliver thought that Jake had a right to know about the child, but Deborah decided at that moment that she would not tell him. It was her own responsibility, she didn't want the help or the pity of a man who did not love her. As she carefully placed her empty coffee cup on the table, she looked at him, and found him staring back, a dark anger in his eyes.

'Why have you been avoiding me?' he asked, holding her glance.

'Have I?'

'You know damn well you have.' The anger was still there, but also a mocking amusement.

Deborah felt her temper boiling up. She didn't find the situation at all amusing. Her nerves were stretched to breaking point and her stomach was churning.

'As far as I'm concerned, if there was ever anything between us, it's over,' she said coldly. 'If I have been avoiding you, it's because I have nothing to say to you.'

Breaking the eye contact, she stood up, moving jerkily to the window.

Jake moved too, swiftly and silently, fury in every line of his body. He caught her arm ungently, spinning her round to face him, his eyes burning into hers.

'Over?' he repeated softly, a cold amusement curving his lips. 'You're carrying my child, Deborah. I'd say that made it far from over, wouldn't you?'

Deborah froze beneath his hands. 'You ... you know! How do you know? How?' He had been playing games with her, and she hated him for that.

'Your stepbrother came to see me this afternoon,' Jake revealed evenly.

'*Oliver?*' She found it almost impossible to believe. 'Why should he tell you?'

Jake released her abruptly, as though he couldn't bear to touch her any longer, turning away and lighting a cigarette. 'He thought I had a right to know. I agreed with him. God knows, I would have waited for ever for you to tell me.'

'He had no right to tell you!' Deborah muttered, burning with the betrayal. She couldn't think of a single reason why Oliver should go behind her back to Jake. It was the last thing she would have suspected. He didn't even like Jake.

'Rights?' Jake laughed, but there was no amusement in the sound. 'You dare to talk of rights?'

Something in his voice cut her to ribbons and she turned on him. 'I want you to go now. I . . . I'm tired and I . . .' The sentence trailed off as he moved towards her, silent and menacing.

She watched the rise and fall of his deep chest as though hypnotised, backing away against the wall.

His voice was quiet yet deadly, as he said, 'When your stepbrother came to see me this afternoon, my first thought was that it was some kind of trick. There's never been any love lost between us——'

'He was only looking after me,' Deborah cut in, her voice shaking. 'There have been times when I've needed protection against you.'

Jake smiled. 'Oh, I'd agree with that. You've always played a dirty game, Deborah, you even had me fooled for quite a while.'

Deborah paled, her eyes burning feverishly. 'You bastard,' she whispered, terribly hurt. He could have invented the double standard, she thought bitterly, longing to hit him, to wipe the smile from his lean dark face, to pierce that thick skin, to get through to him *somehow*.

She saw his mouth tautening into a cruel line. Perhaps she had hit her target after all, she thought with fearful satisfaction.

'I thought that maybe you'd put him up to it,' Jake continued, as though she hadn't spoken. 'It certainly wouldn't have surprised me.'

'Why would I do that?' Deborah asked angrily, smarting from his insults, his low opinon of her.

'I don't know, I couldn't figure it out. I realise now, of course, that you had no damned intention of telling me.' There was a roughness in his voice that had she not known better, she might have interpreted as pain.

'It's not your problem,' she said tiredly, worn out with fighting.

'Don't be ridiculous.' He took her arm, pulling her round, his hand tilting up her face, forcing her to meet his eyes. 'It's my child.'

His casual touch burned her, igniting fires beneath her skin. 'Oh, and what's your advice? Are you going to suggest I get rid of it?' She heard the hiss of his indrawn breath. 'Damn you,' he said harshly, controlling his temper with obvious difficulty.

Their eyes met, hers defiant and fearful, his silvered with anger. The whole room seemed to pulse with electric tension.

'You really think that?' he demanded, expressionlessly.

'Why not? I'm sure this isn't the first time you've had to deal with this . . . this inconvenient situation.' The thought hurt. The thought of him with anyone else hurt like hell and she closed her eyes in case he could read what she was thinking.

Jake let her go, his expression unrevealing. He stared at her downturned face for a moment, then said coolly. 'You have two choices, Deborah. Either you hand the child over to me, when it's born, or you marry me now.'

It was a bombshell, a totally unexpected bombshell.

Suddenly they weren't fighting any more. Jake was hard and cold and single-minded. He was giving her two options and that was all. He was leaving her no room for manoeuvre. Her eyes flew open, the green depths brilliant with shock. 'Marry you?' she whispered in horror.

'That's what I said.' There was mockery in his cool voice.

'You must be joking.' She started to laugh, on the verge of hysteria, totally unaware of how insulting she was being. 'You don't want to marry me, any more than I want to marry you.'

Jake smiled slightly. 'If I were you, I'd think very carefully before refusing.'

'Why?' She still hadn't fully taken it in.

'Because I want that child.' He didn't bother to hide his grim determination and Deborah felt her heart suddenly pounding with fear. She knew how ruthless he could be. He would go to any lengths to get what he wanted. She had seen that for herself.

'I haven't said I'm going to have the baby,' she said wildly, knowing that he was trying to back her into a corner.

Jake's eyes narrowed contemptuously on her face. 'Is that why you sent your stepbrother round to see me. Is it money you want? Money for an abortion?'

'No! No, you know that's not true.' Her bravado dissolved beneath the cold cruelty of his words.

'Why did you say it then? To make me suffer?'

Deborah's green eyes widened. 'How could I make you suffer? You can't pretend that you care.'

Jake was silent for a moment, watching her carefully. 'And if I do?' There was a deep timbre to his voice that was almost her undoing. She didn't understand what he meant.

'It . . . it was a mistake,' she said tautly, close to tears. 'We both know that, and I won't let you trap me. I can have the baby without you. You needn't be involved at all. Oliver should never have told you—I can manage on my own.'

'Perhaps you can,' Jake said very coolly. 'But you won't. My child won't be born a bastard, like I was. You forget that I'm very well acquainted with that aspect of—shall we say—family life.'

Deborah swallowed on the blockage of unshed tears in her throat. She *had* forgotten, and it made her realise the depths of his feelings. Perhaps as a child, he had longed for the father he had never known.

'There's nothing you can do about it,' she said finally, her anger gone.

'I can take you to court, and we can fight it out there,' he told her harshly.

'You wouldn't have a chance of winning!' She was staggered by his heartlessness.

He shrugged. 'Can you be one hundred per cent sure of that?' he queried softly. 'Attitudes and sympathies are changing. But even so, I'm sure such a case would warrant national publicity. I don't imagine Cole Sullivan would be over the moon about that, do you? And you'd need a job to support the child.'

'That's blackmail,' Deborah murmured faintly, hating him. He was deliberately playing on her doubts and insecurities. He surely couldn't win in court. No judge would take her child away from her . . . But as her thoughts ran on, the slight nagging doubt made it impossible to contemplate. Jake was a powerful ruthless man, used to winning. It seemed to her then, that he could do anything he wanted.

'Yes, I guess it is.' He was implacable, as cold as ice.

'How can you do this?' she whispered, sure that he hated her.

His jaw clenched. 'I want my child,' he muttered through his teeth. 'And I'll do anything I have to, I'm giving you fair warning of that, right now.'

Deborah felt the wetness of tears on her face, unable to control them any longer. She heard Jake swearing under his breath, felt the tentacles of his anger reaching out to her. She moved across the room, her arms wrapped defensively around her body.

'You don't leave me with any choice,' she choked, hardly able to contemplate the future.

'You'll marry me?' His voice was quiet, blank.

'I don't know why you're insisting on this! You don't want to marry me,' she prevaricated weakly, trying to control her tears.

Jake shot her a long hard glance. 'No,' he replied at last. 'No, I don't want to marry you, but compared to the child that you're carrying, everything else is irrelevant.'

His detachment made Deborah feel sick. Her mind ran in circles, trying to find an escape route. She loved him, but she would be marrying a man who hated her, a man who was offering marriage only because he wanted to legitimise his unborn child. She didn't think she would be able to bear it.

'Jake, please . . .' She swayed, feeling lightheaded, and he moved quickly, catching her, steadying her, holding her.

'Are you all right?' His eyes were dark with concern, his voice suddenly gentle.

Deborah rested her cheek against his wide shoulder, aching for his comfort, his tenderness, and felt his arms tightening around her.

'I'm fine,' she lied unsteadily. 'Just tired, I suppose.'

The moments ticked by in silence. She felt his calm strength flowing into her veins, giving her life, as she rested against his body.

'Ah, Deborah.' There was an intense weariness in his voice as he said her name. She felt his breath against her hair.

'I didn't want anything from you,' she whispered brokenly.

'You can't fight me for ever, and you can't manage on your own,' he said evenly.

'You're being unreasonable.'

'Maybe.' He was non-committal as he released her, wiping the tears from her face with his fingers. He looked into her eyes. 'We'll be married next week.'

Panic rose in Deborah's throat. 'It's too soon,' she protested fiercely.

'There's no point in putting it off. I'll get the licence tomorrow.' He moved indolently towards the door. 'You should rest,' he suggested with a smile.

Deborah ignored that. 'I won't sleep with you,' she said fiercely. 'If you force me to marry you it will be in name only. I . . . I couldn't bear anything more.'

Jake looked at her, his eyes blank. 'I've told you, it's the child I'm interested in—not you.'

'And when the baby is born, I shall want a divorce,' she told him sharply, his words hurting her more than she could have imagined, cutting straight to her heart.

He nodded. 'As you wish,' he said calmly, making it clear that he couldn't care either way.

'I won't change my mind about that,' Deborah almost shouted, but she was talking to herself. He had already gone.

Alone, she sank down on to the sofa, her legs suddenly giving way under her. He was mad, she thought, as she went over their conversation. And he had won again.

The thought of becoming his wife terrified her, and yet she was forced to admit to herself that it did hold certain attractions. How bad could eight months of anything be? She loved him and although she cursed her own weakness, the thought of living with him was not altogether unpleasant. Perhaps she had abandoned her pride altogether. Letting her hand rest on the flatness of her stomach, she couldn't believe that it was only a few hours since she had confided in Oliver that she might be pregnant. It seemed years ago.

Jake wanted the child, not her, she would have to remember that. He'd agreed to a divorce after the birth. He would keep his word, she was sure. He had made it very clear where his interests lay. She felt tears blurring her vision again. He did not care for her. After eight months he would probably be glad to get rid of her. The outlook for the future was still grim, even though her life had changed so dramatically in the past hours. She felt confused and exhausted, yet strangely more alive than she had felt for a very long time.

It was only half an hour later when she heard the front door slam. Oliver, she thought, getting to her feet. He had some explaining to do. She went downstairs, not bothering to knock as she entered his flat. The place was cluttered as usual, very untidy. Oliver had knocked down the dividing wall between dining room and lounge, leaving a vast amount of space which he had turned into his studio. Canvasses lay everywhere, on easels, stacked on the floor, hung on the walls, and the smell of linseed and turpentine pervaded the air.

He appeared from the kitchen with a coffee pot and a sandwich in his hands, as Deborah picked her way through the artist's debris.

'I'll get another cup,' he said, before she could open her mouth, and disappeared back into the kitchen. She sat down on one of the old velvet chairs that surrounded the ornate iron fireplace. On the mantelpiece stood a beautiful glass lamp, by Galle, moulded in the shape of a giant mushroom. She stared at it, admiring it, as she always did. It was one of Oliver's prized possessions as a sometime collector of Art Nouveau glass.

Her stepbrother appeared moments later with the extra cup and busied himself with the coffee.

'How are you feeling?' he asked lightly, not meeting her eyes.

'Why did you tell Jake?' she countered, getting straight to the point.

'Has he been in touch?'

'You haven't answered the question. Why did you tell him?' she asked again, exasperated.

'Somebody had to,' Oliver smiled.

'You? What gave you the right? You shouldn't have interfered.' Angrily she slammed her cup into the saucer.

'Okay.' Oliver held up his hands in mock defeat. 'I'm sorry. I knew you'd be annoyed. I just felt that you couldn't manage on your own.'

'I could have managed perfectly well without Jake Logan's help.'

'He had a right to know, it's his child too,' Oliver repeated what he had said that morning. 'I didn't want to see you struggling alone. You take too much on yourself, don't you see?'

Knowing that he had her best interests at heart, took some of the wind out of Deborah's sails. 'Well, there's not much chance of my being alone now,' she grumbled, holding out her cup for more coffee.

'Why, what's happened?' Oliver eyed her with undisguised curiosity.

For a moment Deborah was tempted to tell him about Jake's blackmail. But it was not his problem. He could only worry about her, and she didn't want that. 'It looks as though I'll be married this time next week,' she revealed grudgingly.

'Good God!' Oliver tried to hide his shock, by adding hastily, 'Congratulations! That's great news.'

'Is it?'

'Of course it is, you silly girl.' He stood up, searching the cupboards for glasses and whisky. 'We need something stronger to celebrate this.'

Deborah stared at him open mouthed. 'You don't even like him!' she exclaimed. And when he didn't turn round. 'Oliver, are you listening to me? Have you gone mad?'

Oliver turned his head, smiling broadly. 'Actually, I liked him a lot better today. And I've always thought his plays were brilliant.'

'You . . . you traitor!' She could hardly believe her ears. Even Oliver was on Jake's side now. 'If you like him so much, you can marry him,' she said, her green eyes glinting.

'You don't want to get married?' Oliver's smile was devilish.

'No—yes—no, of course I don't,' she stumbled damningly.

The smile grew wider. 'Why not? You love him, don't you?'

There was nothing Deborah could say to that.

CHAPTER EIGHT

THE wedding ceremony was a quiet affair with only Oliver and Tess as witnesses.

Deborah felt numb as she heard Jake's deep voice taking the vows, her hand trembling as he slid the heavy gold band on to her wedding finger. Her own voice seemed too high, hardly recognisable as she promised to love and honour until she died.

She was dressed in cream silk, paid for by Jake at his insistence. Inside, the designer label was explanation enough for the beautiful cut. It was simple in style, flowing over the curves of her body, with satin embroidery around the low neck. The loose matching jacket was also embroidered, the silk smooth and sensual against her skin. Around her neck lay a necklace of emeralds, rubies and diamonds set in gold, another present from Jake. It was exquisitely beautiful, heavy and cold against her throat. He had given it to her the day before the wedding, his eyes cool and expressionless. And although she had refused to accept it, he had insisted, brushing aside her protests until she had to give in.

She glanced at him now from beneath the sweep of her lashes, and her breath caught painfully. He was wearing a dark, expensively cut suit, his white shirt immaculate, his black hair brushed back from the hard lines of his face. He seemed calm and remote, a powerful, attractive stranger.

As the ceremony ended, he turned and touched her mouth with his own. It was a brief kiss, over before

Deborah realised his intention. Her startled eyes met his, and the cool mockery she saw in his face brought the colour pouring into her cheeks.

They left the building to drive to Jake's house where a reception party had been arranged. She felt the weight of his arm around her shoulders, and shivered, somehow hurt by the careless intimacy. What have I done, she thought in panic. What the hell have I done?

As they stepped into the cold April air, they were confronted by a battery of clicking cameras, and the dazzling brightness of flashguns. Somebody was calling Jake's name, questions buzzing around them. Deborah stood dazed for a second, jostled and pushed by the reporters, bombarded with questions, some insultingly personal, until Jake guided her quickly into his car. He drove away without hesitation, leaving the small crowd of people still moving, still taking photographs.

'Are you all right?' He glanced at her and she nodded. 'Who the hell tipped them off?' he wondered irritably, as they reached the edge of the city.

'Don't look at me,' she retorted, smoothing back her hair. Jake was obviously very newsworthy, used to the attention, but it was the first time it had happened to her and she still felt a little shocked by the pushing, the demanding questions and avid curiosity. They reminded her of vultures, fighting for blood.

She glanced surreptitiously at Jake's profile and found it hard and expressionless. She looked down at the heavy gold band on her finger, playing with it nervously. She didn't know him at all. There were so many sides to his character. She couldn't possibly guess what he was thinking now. Worry prickled down her spine, and she shivered.

'Cold?' He picked up on it immediately, averting his eyes from the road for a second.

'No, frightened, I suppose,' she answered truthfully.

'About what?'

'You know damn well!' She turned away, staring out of the window at the grey clouds scudding low across the sky. Jake was silent for a moment, then he said, 'You're not a child, Deborah, don't act like one.'

'I didn't want to get married,' she glared at him, hurt by his coldness, knowing that she sounded like the child he accused her of being.

'Sulking won't change the situation,' he said, but he was smiling, a quality of tenderness in his voice.

Deborah felt her heart lurching painfully, and lapsed into silence for the rest of the journey.

Everybody was waiting for them when they arrived. The house was full of people. Deborah took a glass of champagne and found herself swallowed up in the crowd. People she didn't know, rushed over, congratulating her and Jake. Beautiful, impeccably-dressed women eyed her up and down assessingly. No doubt wondering how she had managed to capture the interest of a man like Jake, she thought wryly, as she fended off their pointed questions. Hands caught her waist from behind, and turning, she found herself face to face with Cole.

'Great party,' he said, but he wasn't smiling. 'I suppose congratulations are in order.'

'You don't approve?' she parried lightly, her eyes smiling into his.

'What do you think? Three years ago, I helped throw that guy out, remember? I saw what he did to you last time you got involved with him.'

Deborah lowered her eyes, knowing with a rush of

sadness, that all Cole's bitterness stemmed from jealousy.

She remembered that balmy night on Corfu, when he had almost told her how he felt about her. It seemed a million years ago, as though it had happened to a different person. 'I love him,' she said gently, hoping that Cole would understand.

'I know. You don't have to spell it out, it's written all over your face.'

'I wish . . . I wish you could be happy for me,' she said quietly.

'That's asking too much, sweetheart.' He threw back the whisky in his glass, grabbing another from the tray of a passing waiter. 'And you know damn well why.'

'Don't.' She touched his arm, her eyes pleading.

'Don't what? Is my beautiful young wife begging favours, Sullivan?' Jake's cool hard voice cut between them, and Deborah found him beside her. How long had he been standing there, she wondered. Had he heard it all? His eyes were clear and ice cold, his chill glance sweeping from Cole to Deborah.

Cole laughed, but his eyes held nervousness as though he had picked up the barely veiled threat in Jake's careless remark. 'I'm just lamenting the loss of the best designer I ever had on the books.'

'It won't be forever,' Deborah said soothingly. 'After I've had the baby, I'll be able to work from home. And until then, you know very well that Cassandra can take my place. Her work is brilliant and she's been waiting ages for a chance like this.'

Cole smiled. 'You keep telling me that, so I guess I have to believe it.' He looked at Jake. 'You're a very lucky man.'

'I know,' Jake replied, the words perfectly courteous

but delivered with an edge of ice. He slid his arm around Deborah's shoulders, and guided her away.

'You were so rude to him,' she accused, as soon as they were out of earshot.

'He's drunk,' Jake said, shooting her a narrowed, probing look. 'Why, I wonder?'

'I don't know what you mean.' She averted her eyes, colour staining her cheeks.

Jake's glance became speculative, his mouth a hard straight line. 'I mean that it's out of character.'

Deborah didn't comment, and he said, 'Was your relationship with him more than just professional?'

Flustered, she retorted, 'That's a terrible thing to suggest.' She felt angry at his perception. He looked at Cole and saw everything.

'And that doesn't answer my question.' The grey eyes held hers in cold silent demand.

Defeated, she gave in. 'I'm very fond of Cole,' she said quietly. 'But we're not lovers. It's never been like that.'

Jake smiled, a triumphant gleam in his eyes. 'He's in love with you.'

'I hope not.' She didn't want to hurt Cole, although she knew in her heart that Jake was right. Why did love always hurt?

'Dance with me,' Jake said softly, sensing her unhappiness.

'I don't want to dance.' For some reason she felt belligerent, close to tears, her emotions in turmoil.

'You're going to anyway. It's expected of us,' he told her in a clipped voice, his face brooking no argument as he took her in his arms. As they moved to the music, Deborah let her head rest against his wide shoulder. She felt the hard strength of his body against her own, and a dizzying weakness filled her.

Did they look like a couple deeply involved with each other, she wondered painfully. Did they look like lovers? The idea was too attractive to be in any way amusing, and she stopped her thoughts in their tracks, letting her mind drift, allowing her body to move instinctively with Jake's to the soft music.

The party drifted on, and Deborah drank far too much champagne in an effort to get through it all in one piece. She began to feel lightheaded, almost happy, falling into the gay spirit of the party. On her way down the wide polished staircase, after checking her hair, and make-up, she suddenly found Leila blocking her way. Neither girl smiled. Leila had obviously just arrived, a black woollen coat slung over her arm. She was beautiful, Deborah had to admit, her black hair pulled back from her sculptured face and held in a diamond clip, her dress black chiffon that revealed every curve of her perfect figure and long legs.

As the silence lengthened, Deborah decided that she had to break it. 'Hello, Leila,' she said coolly. 'How are you?'

Leila didn't answer, her eyes on the gold wedding ring on Deborah's finger.

'I suppose you think you've been very clever,' she finally said, her face suddenly full of hatred, her voice heavily accented in anger.

Deborah saw that hatred and recoiled from it. 'What . . . what are you talking about?' she asked faintly. To be confronted with such intense hostility had thrown her off balance.

'You——' Leila replied acidly. 'I'm talking about you, somehow managing to trick Jake into marriage.'

'Now just a minute——' Deborah began, but Leila cut her off.

'How did you do it?' she demanded, her black eyes burning. 'How on earth could you have managed it? The oldest trick in the book, perhaps? Have you told him that you're pregnant?'

She had hit on the truth purely by accident, but Deborah felt herself flushing, giving herself away.

Leila laughed, a high hysterical laugh. 'You won't get away with it. You won't last five minutes. Jake belongs to me,' she said, misinterpreting Deborah's reaction.

'Excuse me.' Sickened by the venom she heard in Leila's voice, Deborah tried to walk away, but the other girl caught her arm, her long red nails digging spitefully into Deborah's skin. 'Don't make yourself too comfortable here,' she advised viciously. 'I did it once and I'll do it again. You'll be out of this house within the month, I can promise you——' She stopped, her eyes focusing over Deborah's shoulder. 'Jake, darling...' She let go of Deborah and rushed towards Jake, who was strolling towards them. She flung her arms around his neck, her mood completely different, smiling as she reached up to kiss his mouth.

Deborah watched wide-eyed, astonished. From spitting poison one second, Leila had changed, now warm and smiling as she stared up into Jake's grey eyes.

'You're late,' he said indulgently, untangling her arms from around his neck and gently pushing her away.

'I know. Forgive me, I was delayed.' Her voice was sweet and pleading, childlike.

'You called the newspapers, didn't you?' Jake said, but there was no anger in his voice.

'Did I?' Leila laughed, pleased with herself.

Deborah turned away in disgust. Obviously Leila

was still in love with Jake, even though she believed him that they were no longer lovers.

She heard Jake calling her name as she wandered back into the party, but she ignored him, her mind spinning with Leila's threats, her vicious anger. To Deborah, she had seemed unbalanced, on the verge of a breakdown. She could feel sympathy but she still couldn't like her.

'There you are!' Tess' voice broke into her troubled thoughts. 'I've been looking for you for ages. Where's Jake?'

'He's in the hall with Leila,' Deborah replied, trying to keep her voice expressionless.

'Oh, but . . .' Tess seemed about to say something, then thought better of it. She took Deborah's arm, squeezing it affectionately. 'I'm so happy for you both.' Her smile grew confidential. 'And I've got a confession to make.'

Deborah found herself smiling too. 'What is it?'

'My birthday party. I was matchmaking,' Tess admitted without remorse.

'Really? I'd never have guessed!' Deborah laughed, partly at the irony of it all.

'I had to tell you,' Tess said, her eyes very bright. 'You were obviously made for each other and you were both so miserable.'

Deborah couldn't believe that Jake had ever been miserable without her. Tess was just an incurable romantic.

'What about you?' she asked, changing the subject.

'There's nobody special, but I haven't given up hope.'

There was an untouched longing on her face, and Deborah thought sadly, I must have looked like that once.

The party broke up late and it was after midnight when the last guests drifted away. Alone with Jake in the lounge, Deborah stared into the flames of the roaring fire and felt her heart beating too quickly. It was a beautiful comfortable room with pale magnolia walls, thick jewel-bright carpets and sofas covered with lightly-patterned chintz.

Two silk covered lamps threw pools of intimate light across the room and on a low carved table stood the tray of coffee Daisy had brought in five minutes earlier. The silence was broken only by the quiet ticking of the old wooden clock on the mantelpiece and the cracking of the logs on the fire. The tray had been left near Deborah and she leaned over to it now.

'Do you want coffee?' she asked, and her voice sounded high and breathless.

Jake looked at her, his eyes very dark. 'Yes, thank you.'

Deborah poured from the silver pot. 'Cream, sugar?' she asked unnecessarily.

The dark grey eyes held hers. 'You know how I take my coffee,' he said quietly.

Without answering, she handed him the delicate china cup. Yes, she knew how he took his coffee. Strong and black with no sugar, he drank gallons of the stuff. She remembered everything she had ever learned about him, every tiny detail. And that depressed her. She drank her own coffee, her fingers shaking around the cup.

Around them the house was silent. She had offered to help Daisy with the clearing up, but the housekeeper had assured her that the hired staff were seeing to it all, and there was absolutely nothing she could do.

She felt tired. The day had been a long one,

stretching her nerves. She felt restless too. She didn't know how she should act with Jake. She didn't know what was expected of her.

In making the arrangements for the wedding, he had consulted her, wanting to know her opinions. She had refused to co-operate, still angry, telling him to get on with it himself. He had done just that, and she wished now that she had taken an active interest. At the time, she had been defiant. By not knowing any of the details, the wedding had seemed less real. She could pretend that it wasn't happening. It had been another mistake.

She looked at Jake and found him watching her, his expression veiled. In the soft light his face was shadowed and she felt the powerful magnetism of his attraction, pulling her against her will.

He smiled lazily. 'You look serious?'

She shrugged. 'It's a been a long day.' She was non-committal, fighting a sudden and almost over-powering urge to go to him and beg him to make love to her.

She looked away and said, 'Caroline Winters wasn't at the party.'

'No.' He was as non-committal as she had been.

'You didn't invite her?' Something forced her to ask. Examining her need to know, she found that she was jealous, fiercely jealous of every woman Jake showed an interest in, every woman he looked at.

'She wouldn't have come.' He looked at her, mockery in his smile.

'Why? Are you and she——?' She broke off, biting her lip. Did she really want to know? Did she have the right to ask?

'Lovers?' Jake supplied calmly. Deborah nodded, averting her eyes from the lean hardness of his face.

Although she was frightened of the truth, she found she did want to know.

'Is it important?' His voice revealed nothing.

'Yes,' she whispered, uncaring of what she betrayed, her green eyes finding his.

Jake was silent as he searched her face, then he said. 'We had a brief affair about a year ago. She's a good actress, she's worked in a few of my plays. We're still friends, nothing more.'

On his part, Deborah realised with a flash of intuition. Caroline Winters hadn't been at the party because she still wanted Jake.

'Oh I see,' she said lightly, trying to hide her relief.

'Do you?' Jake's mouth twisted. 'I doubt it.'

Something in his voice warned her to drop the subject before she found herself in too deep. She stood up, moving restlessly around the room. 'Let's talk about something else,' she suggested pretending interest in a large abstract painting, hanging on one of the walls.

'What do you suggest?' Jake watched her as she moved, slender and graceful, the silk dress clinging to the softness of her body.

She shrugged, frowning. 'I don't know. Anything.' The room seemed filled with tension and she felt the hair on the back of her neck prickling.

'Okay. Let's talk about you and me,' he said softly.

Her head jerked round and she eyed him warily. 'What about you and me?'

'Tomorrow we're flying out to Seville,' he informed her with a slight smile.

'Seville? Why?' She felt suspicious, nervous. What was he up to?

Jake stood up in one lithe movement and walked over to her. He was so tall she had to tilt back her head to look into his face.

'The play I'm writing at the moment has its roots in the Spanish Civil War. I need to do some research.' He reached out slowly, his long fingers stroking her hair. 'And you need a holiday. I know these past weeks have been a strain for you.'

Deftly he removed the pins that held her hair in place, so that it fell loose and shining about her shoulders. 'You look tired,' he said gently. Trembling violently beneath his touch, she tried to move away but he trapped her against the wall, his hands resting either side of her.

'I am tired,' she admitted, and her voice sounded sharp, a defence against his unexpected kindness.

It was true. The wedding had exhausted her, coming after weeks of solidly hard work. Since returning from Windermere she had thrown herself into her work, catching up on the backlog and finishing her designs for the new collection. The past week had been spent grooming Cassandra to take her place. All her strength seemed used up, and the thought of a holiday was enticing, though the thought of sharing that holiday with Jake made her heart pound with worry.

'But I won't let you bully me. I don't need a holiday.'

'You'll have one anyway,' Jake told her smoothly, his voice implacable. 'Call it a honeymoon if you like.'

'No!' It was an involuntary rejection. 'Jake, for God's sake . . .' She watched his mouth hardening, a muscle flicking in his jaw and realised that she had insulted him in her panic. He was so close that she could feel the coolness of his breath against her loosened hair, and that treacherous weakness ran in her blood, undermining her willpower, her self-control.

'Why are you doing this?' she asked, lowering her eyes.

Jake caught her chin between his fingers and tilted up her face. 'Because I want you,' he said calmly.

The ground beneath her feet seemed to move, the words shuddering through her.

'But I don't want you,' she lied, moistening her dry lips with her tongue, an unknowingly provocative gesture.

Jake smiled, but his eyes were smoky, heavy with desire. 'You're my wife,' he reminded her in a low voice.

'Because you blackmailed me.' Her voice cracked. The tension snaked between them like raw electricity, blotting out the rest of the world. She was acutely aware of him, her mind and her body open to him, sensitive, achingly alive.

'It was your own decision,' he muttered angrily.

'Liar!' She tried to pull away from him, but she couldn't move a muscle. She was paralysed by the naked desire she saw in his face.

'You really think I'd have taken you to court?'

'Yes,' she whispered, her heart racing. 'Yes.'

Very gently, Jake traced the outline of her parted lips with his thumb. She shuddered uncontrollably.

'You're the liar,' he said, and there was a teasing tenderness in his voice.

Slowly he bent his dark head, his mouth finding hers, tormenting her with brief hungry kisses that parted her lips then broke away. Unable to keep her balance, her hands came up flat against his shoulders. Beneath the thin material of his shirt, she felt the smooth hard warmth of his skin, the tension in his powerful muscles. And she swayed against him, weak with longing, her sudden need matching the need she felt in him. His arms came around her, holding her tightly against the length of his body.

'You're driving me out of my mind,' he murmured, his voice rough with emotion, his mouth sliding to her throat. 'God, Deborah, I want you—I don't think a lifetime could ease this pain . . .'

Deborah closed her eyes, her hands still caressing his wide muscular shoulders, tangling in the vital thickness of his hair. She knew how he felt. She wanted him with an intensity that made her feel faint.

'I want you,' she whispered, her voice breaking. It was not an admission of defeat, but an answering of his need. 'Jake, hold me, please, hold me.'

She felt the strength of his arms tightening possessively around her, and, suddenly the wetness of tears on her face. She swallowed them back, aware that she was on the point of abandoning her foolish pride for ever. She would never know a love like this again.

Unbidden, Leila's face rose in her mind, holding her back, reminding her that Jake had never loved her.

'Why . . . why did Leila tell the press?' she asked in a shaking voice.

Jake stared down into her face, his grey eyes still heavy with desire. 'God knows,' he said huskily. 'I guess because she's not very well. She can't always——'

'Three years ago, I found her in your bed,' Deborah cut in, unbearably hurt because he was still defending Leila, even now. 'I don't think you can excuse that by saying she wasn't very well, damn you!'

She felt him stiffen, his body tensing. The desire faded from his eyes, his face becoming a hard expressionless mask. 'What the hell are you talking about?' he demanded.

'You know very well,' Deborah almost shouted.

'You must have thought I was a fool, and I suppose I was to have trusted you.'

She saw his jaw clenching. He grabbed her, his hands bruising the fragile bones of her shoulders.

'Tell me,' he said harshly.

'You don't remember?' All the pain that she had been holding in for three long years seemed to spill out unchecked. She felt angrier than she had ever felt before in her life. 'No, I don't suppose you do. I came here to see you. I went upstairs to your room and found Leila in your bed. You were in the shower. I *hated* you!' She spat the words at him, her eyes wild.

Jake's grip on her shoulders tightened until she thought her bones would break. She winced with pain.

'And I hate you now!' she added, struggling against his hands.

'So you went straight to Stevens,' Jake muttered, between his teeth.

'What difference does it make?'

He let her go, releasing her so abruptly that she nearly fell. They stood inches apart, suddenly facing each other as bitter enemies. He was breathing heavily, his hands clenched into fists at his sides, his eyes leaping with fury.

'You stupid little bitch. I've never taken Leila to bed, I've never touched her.'

'You're a liar!' Deborah said wildly. 'A *liar!*' She flew at him, beating at his broad chest with her fists, wanting to kill him. 'I saw you with my own eyes.'

He caught her hands, pinioning them behind her back, pulling her against his hard body.

She fought him violently as he began to kiss her. His mouth was angry, almost brutal and she tried to resist. But her body betrayed her again, her lips parting almost immediately, her response quick and fierce.

Jake let go of her hands and they crept up around his neck, to touch his hair, his shoulders. She moaned beneath the demanding hunger of his mouth.

At last he lifted his head and stared down into her hot blind face, bitterness in his eyes.

'How could you go to him? How could you let him touch you?' The words were torn from him, harsh and accusing.

'I didn't.' She felt too weary to lie any more. She closed her eyes, lowering her head.

'*What?*' He tilted up her face, hurting her, forcing her to look at him.

'I didn't,' she repeated, dry mouthed, knowing she had to tell him the truth. 'I never did. Robert was never my lover.'

Jake's grey eyes held hers, searching her face. 'I saw you together.'

'He loved me. That night you saw us, I didn't expect him to kiss me, I didn't want him to. As far as I was concerned we were just old friends. I never thought of him any other way. Never.' There was a calm relief in finally telling him the truth. 'I didn't see him for months after that night.'

'Your stepbrother told me——'

'It was to protect me. I didn't want to see you.'

Jake's mouth hardened, his jaw tense. 'You married him, dammit.'

'Because he was dying. It was what he wanted and I couldn't refuse him,' she whispered, the tears coursing down her face.

Jake swore long and violently. His face was white, totally blank. His eyes were burning like fire.

'Jake, I . . .' She had to say something. She was

disturbed by what she saw in him.

He didn't look at her. He turned away and walked from the room in silence, his body very tense. Deborah watched him go in confusion, not understanding his anger, his deathly fury.

Her mind was in a turmoil, refusing to function properly. She sank down on to a chair and cried her eyes out.

CHAPTER NINE

THEY arrived in Seville at eight o'clock the following evening. Deborah slept for most of the flight, her head resting on Jake's shoulder.

She woke as the plane touched the runway, embarrassed colour flushing her cheeks as she lifted her head and met Jake's dark eyes.

'What time is it?' She smoothed back her hair, feeling hot and tired, needing something to say.

'Just after eight.' He was watching her, his face unfathomable.

She turned away, looking through the tiny window. Outside it was very dark, she couldn't see a thing as the plane slowed. 'I must have been asleep since we left Valencia,' she said quickly, still embarrassed that she had woken in his arms.

Jake smiled at her nervous chatter, and lowering his head, kissed her briefly on the mouth.

She looked at him, wide-eyed with surprise, her fingers coming up to touch her lips, but he was already moving, reaching for her jacket, handing it to her.

Most of the other first class passengers had left the plane at Valencia. Seville airport terminal was small and deserted and they cleared customs quickly.

A small knot of people waited behind the thin partition outside. A tall dark man shouted Jake's name. Jake answered in rapid Spanish, leading Deborah towards the man who was standing with his arm round a slender dark-haired woman. He introduced them as Concepción and Fernando Garcia de Loza.

Deborah smiled, shaking hands. Fernando was tall and distinguished. She guessed he was in his early forties, very attractive, his face tanned and strong. His wife Concepción was younger, very beautiful, with long raven hair plaited down her back.

'You must call me Conchi, everybody does,' she said, her English perfect. She took Deborah's arm as they stepped out into the warm night air.

Concepción and Fernando were leaving on a three month business trip to Hong Kong the following day. Knowing that Jake needed peace to work on his play, they had offered the use of their house while they were away. Fernando was an old friend. He and Jake had attended the same university, Fernando now being a very rich, very successful antique dealer with an international reputation.

At the kerb outside stood a long black limousine, a driver holding open the doors.

Deborah breathed in deeply, enjoying the night air with its distinctly Continental scent.

'Is this your first visit to Spain?' Concepción asked, noticing Deborah's interest in everything around her.

Deborah nodded, her eyes shining. 'And I think I'm going to like it.'

Fernando watched her face as she spoke, his dark eyes openly admiring. He turned to Jake. 'You are a very lucky man, my friend. *Dios*, but your new wife is beautiful.'

'I know,' Jake said softly, his eyes serious as he looked at her. Something in his voice made Deborah's heart lurch violently. She knew that it was all an act for the benefit of Concepción and Fernando, but she couldn't help responding. I'm a fool, she thought, turning away to look out of the window.

The airport was some miles from the centre of the city, but the drive was pleasant, the road wide and empty. Jake and Fernando talked in English as a courtesy to Deborah, and it was obvious that they were close friends, strong bonds of affection and respect binding them together.

As they approached the centre of the City, the traffic became heavier.

Concepción and Fernando's house was near the Guadalquivir River, on the edge of the Bario Santa Cruz. It was a large old building, Moorish in style, barely visible from the road.

The car pulled through high ornate iron gates into a huge tiled courtyard, filled with exotic plants, orange trees and the splashing sounds of a fountain.

Deborah stepped out of the car, looking round with an exclamation of delight. The night air was warm and inviting, the scent of jasmine, orange blossom and carnation filling her nostrils. Birds sang in wooden cages, and from somewhere far away drifted the sound of a plaintive flamenco guitar.

'It's beautiful . . . breathtaking.' She looked round and found Jake beside her. He smiled down into her green eyes, his mouth sensual.

'I'm glad you like it.'

There was mockery in his voice, reminding her of her stubbornness about coming here. But there was tenderness too, and for a moment they were totally alone, a deep awareness binding them together.

'You'll want to rest before dinner.' Concepción's laughing voice broke between them, her high-heeled shoes clattering on the rainbow-coloured tiles. 'I'll show you to your room. Leave the cases, Joaquim will bring them directly.'

The house flanked the rectangular courtyard on all four sides, and Concepión led them through a high arched door of heavily carved oak, into a hallway the size of Deborah's flat in London.

The floor was pale polished marble. All around the hall archways led to rooms hidden behind high carved doors. The architecture was spacious and graceful, everywhere a profusion of old Moroccan tiles, their faded colours glowing beneath crystal lanterns.

Upstairs, Concepción threw open a door, gesturing them inside. 'I hope you'll be comfortable here. I'll send Ana up with some coffee. Dinner in two hours?'

Deborah smiled gratefully. 'Thank you.'

'No, thank you, we are happy to have you here with us,' Concepción said graciously, her liquid dark eyes on Jake, as she added teasingly, 'we were beginning to think that Jake would never find the woman he wanted to spend the rest of his life with. I've been dying to meet you.'

She left them as Joaquim appeared with their luggage. He was a middle-aged man with a dried brown face. He smiled at Deborah, flashing gold teeth, as he retreated silently from the room.

Deborah glanced round as the door closed. It was a beautiful room, decorated luxuriously with the antiques of Fernando's trade.

A carved bed with a canopy of midnight blue velvet dominated the room. The windows, on opposite walls, were open, delicate fretwork shutters pulled across, to keep out insects. Two doors revealed a dressing room and an *en suite* bathroom with a huge marble bath and blue and gold tiles.

The coffee arrived before Deborah had finished looking round. She sipped it gratefully, realising she was very thirsty. She pushed open the shutters to stare out into the balmy night.

The house backed on to the gardens of the Alcazar, the palm trees tall against the black sky. From the other window across the room the view was the terracotta tiled roofs of the Bario.

'It's like going back in time,' she said turning her head to find Jake watching her unsmilingly. The sudden realisation that they were alone in this exquisite room, robbed her of further speech, and she could hear her own heart beating in the silence.

Jake had removed his jacket. His shirt was open at the neck, revealing fine dark hair against tanned skin.

She stared at his wide muscular shoulders, and her mouth dried, her throat aching with sudden tension. The cup she was holding rattled in its saucer. She set it down, very carefully. 'There's only one bed,' she realised shakily.

'You've noticed.' There was amusement in the deep voice.

'But . . .' She tried to find the right words, angry that he was laughing at her. 'You tricked me——'

'On the contrary. I suppose Conchi and Fernando assumed that our marriage is a normal one,' Jake said sardonically. 'One room. One bed.'

'I won't sleep with you, I told you that. I can't.' Panic made her unwittingly rude, and Jake's mouth hardened.

'I suggest you go and tell Conchi that. Ask her for another room.'

It was clear that he was not going to help her and the thought of explaining to Concepción that she couldn't share a room with her husband, was too embarrassing to contemplate. Her mind worked fast. Tomorrow the house would be theirs. She could sleep where she liked then. But until then, she would have to manage somehow.

'I think I'll take a shower before dinner,' she said coolly, shooting him a poisonous glance.

'Running away?' Jake queried mockingly.

'No. I feel hot and sticky after the flight. I don't really enjoy flying.' She hated her own transparency. Jake looked at her and she could hide nothing. And she had to stop herself from running into the bathroom to get away from those penetrating all-seeing eyes.

In the shower she let the warm water sluice over her. She soaped her body and shampooed her hair, letting her mind drift back over the events of the past two days.

She was glad that Jake finally knew the truth about Robert. Telling him had lifted a great weight from her shoulders. Why had he been so furious, though? She would have expected his reaction to be very different. Amusement or triumph but not anger. Her admission hadn't changed anything between them, though. Last night she had tossed and turned in Jake's wide bed, not wanting to be alone, aching for him. He had slept elsewhere because she had woken alone as well. Even now she felt that deep ache in the centre of her body. She recognised her desire with reluctant dismay. Why had he lied about Leila? Her eyes had not deceived her. How could he deny it so coolly, so implacably?

She sighed heavily. So many questions and not one satisfactory answer. It seemed they had reached a tense stalemate, and she could see no way out of it. Even loving him so desperately, she couldn't forgive him, she couldn't trust him. She had been hurt too much, by a man who obviously didn't love her.

Her mouth straightened. There was no point in

going over it again and again. It got her nowhere. As she reluctantly reached to turn off the tap, the lights flickered and failed, plunging her into complete darkness.

She cried out, alarmed, not realising that she was calling Jake's name. He was there in a second, and as he pulled back the shower curtain, the lights came on again with sudden startling brightness.

'The lights . . .' she stammered, feeling very foolish.

'The electricity supply here can be pretty erratic,' he explained, as his eyes met hers.

'Oh, I . . .' She couldn't think of anything to say, freezing into immobility as she read the expression burning in his face.

'You're all right? You didn't fall?' He sounded concerned, and she felt her heart glowing, until she remembered that it was probably the baby he was worried about, not her.

'No, I'm fine, thank you.' Her voice was sharp with disappointment.

Jake smiled, reading her mind, his glittering eyes moving down over her wet naked body in slow intimate appraisal.

Those eyes were hypnotic, possessive, and to her shame, she could feel herself responding as though he was physically touching her.

Her breasts ached, the nipples hardening, the muscles in her stomach becoming taut. The water from the shower still washed over her, making her skin gleam like pearl. Jake's unhurried gaze finally returned to her flushed face.

'You're beautiful,' he said huskily, the curve of his mouth fiercely sensual. Deborah stared at him, unable to say a word. He picked up one of the thick towels that lay over the side of the bath, and held it out for her. With shaking fingers, she turned off the water and stepped out, allowing him to wrap the towel around her, sarong-like. He turned her to face him, his arms still holding her. She smiled into his smoky grey eyes, aware of her bare shoulders still gleaming with water, her hair curling damply around her white throat, and heard the harsh intake of his breath. A sweet sexual awareness buzzed between them, almost a tangible force. They stared into each other's eyes, and she felt his slight hesitation.

'Don't treat me like a child,' she said in a low voice, not thinking with her head, but obeying the pure emotion that was spiralling inside her.

Jake didn't answer, but lifted her in his strong arms until her face was on a level with his, her feet not touching the floor.

She gazed at the firm, beautifully moulded line of his mouth, waiting for its touch with impatient longing. He did not move, and obeying her instincts, she leaned forward and kissed him tentatively, touching his mouth with her lips. She felt his body tensing, the muscles tightening, and realised when she looked into his eyes, that this was the first time she had kissed him since their parting. It had always been him who had made the first move.

She kissed him again, brushing his mouth with gentle delicacy. He didn't respond for a second. Then, with a groan that seemed to come from his very soul, his mouth possessed hers, forcing her to kiss him deeply, parting her lips, showing her the need he could no longer conceal.

The towel fell unnoticed to the marble floor. Jake's hands slid gently over her wet skin. He caressed her slowly, stroking, exploring her body with the sure possessive touch of a lover, his strong fingers familiar with every curve, every hollow, knowing how to give her pleasure.

And still he kissed her, deeper and deeper, with more demand, drugging her with his passion and with a mindless burning sweetness that made her tremble against him.

Then he lifted her into his arms, as though she was no lighter than a feather, carrying her easily to the velvet-covered bed, and gently laying her down. He arched over her, and their mouths fused again.

Deborah fumbled with the buttons of his shirt, until the hard warmth of his chest lay beneath her shaking fingers. She caressed the hair-roughened skin, the smooth power of his shoulders, delighting in his responsive shudder.

He was beautiful, she thought achingly, his body hard and pure and powerfully masculine. Beneath her gentle hands she could feel the heavy pounding of his heart, proof, if she needed any, that he wanted her as desperately as she wanted him. It was a sweet power to hold. She could arouse him with a touch, a kiss, a caress. She let her mouth drift tenderly over his chest, breathing in the clean erotic scent of his skin. He groaned, his body unbearably tense, filmed with perspiration. He reached for her, framing her face between his hands, searching her eyes. 'Deborah.' Her name came unevenly from his lips. 'Oh, God, Deborah.'

The words seemed to break the spell, bringing her to her senses, finally penetrating the desire that had blinded coherent thought.

What was she doing, allowing him to make love to her like this? She had encouraged him, almost begged for his touch. What would he think? That any time he wanted her, she would be more than willing?

She stiffened in his arms. She wouldn't let him use her. He didn't believe in fidelity, and she had no intention of letting him hurt her again. If they became lovers, she would only be one of many, and she couldn't bear the thought.

She had to hold part of herself back from him for her own protection.

'No.' She turned her head away in sudden anguish, struggling against his hands.

He let her go easily, his dark brows drawing together in a frown. Deborah felt herself shivering, tears filling her eyes, her emotions at fever pitch. She had made a fool of herself, and had probably given herself away. Did he know that she loved him? The thought was unendurable.

All desire was gone, doused with humiliation. She felt cold and stiff and vulnerable. How could she offer everything she had so freely to a man who didn't love her? Was she so eager to become just another woman in the long line of women willing to satisfy his needs? She lay sobbing, curled up with her back to him.

'Deborah, what is it?' His voice was gentle and concerned, still husky with passion. He reached out and touched her bare shoulder when she didn't answer, and she flinched away.

'Let me go,' she muttered tearfully. 'Don't touch me.'

'That's quite a change,' he said coolly. He didn't release her, but used his strength to turn her, so that she faced him.

'Leave me alone!' She refused to lift her head, wrapping her arms around her naked body, shivering.

He stared down at her with unfathomable eyes. 'Why are you crying?' he asked quietly, then, seeing she was shivering, handed her a thick towelling robe from the end of the bed. 'Here, put this on, for God's sake.'

Deborah got off the bed and gratefully slipped into it. She tried to pull herself together, swallowing back her tears, wiping her face.

Jake watched her in silence. He could guess why she had frozen in his arms. She still couldn't trust him. She looked frail and vulnerable in the white robe, and so beautiful, she tore at his heart. His body ached for the satisfaction only she could give him, but he knew that he would have to be patient. He could arouse her, he was fully aware of that, he could take her now, if he reached for her. But if he did that, he would lose her, perhaps for ever, and he couldn't take the chance.

Three years had been long enough—too damned long! This time there would be no compromise, no mistakes. She wasn't a child any more and he wanted her more than he had ever wanted a woman in his life. He couldn't let her go again. He pushed a hand through his hair, and realised how tense he was. He forced his body to relax. Sexual satisfaction wasn't enough. He wanted everything, and that meant he would have to go slowly.

Deborah, glancing at him from beneath her lashes, could read no expression at all in his face. He seemed calm and controlled, as always. As though desire had not touched him, as though the events of the last half hour had not happened.

She pushed back her tousled hair. I must look an utter mess, she thought miserably. The white robe was far too big, her eyes were red and swollen, her mouth bruised. She couldn't imagine Leila ever looking a mess ... Disturbed by her own thoughts, she started moving, intending to wash her face in the bathroom.

Jake's voice halted her. 'Where are you going?'

She didn't look at him. 'I'm going to get dressed for dinner,' she said dully.

'Not until we've talked.' He moved silently, suddenly in front of her, blocking her way. His shirt still hung open, revealing the hard lines of his chest, evidence of the desire that had flared between them, still unsatisfied.

She looked up into his cool grey eyes, and saw that the desire still lingered. She knew that her own eyes told him the same. He was not as controlled as he seemed, which somehow made her feel a little better.

'Why were you crying?' he asked again.

She swallowed painfully. 'I was ashamed.'

'Ashamed?' He frowned. 'Of what? Of wanting me?'

'I didn't want you,' she retorted, stung. 'I'll never want you.'

He smiled. 'You're such a beautiful little liar,' he said softly, amused by her childish denial.

'Why should I be?' she demanded, knowing that she wasn't fooling him for a moment. 'You judge everybody by your own low standards.'

'I've never lied to you,' he said, his shoulders strangely tense. 'Never.'

She tried to move away, but he still blocked her path to the sanctuary of the bathroom. It would be so easy to believe him, she thought with wonder. She *wanted* to believe him. The only thing that stood in her way was the evidence of her own eyes, and she couldn't deny that.

'You agreed that this ridiculous marriage would be in name only,' she reminded him, her green eyes flashing defiance.

'And so it is,' Jake mocked, his mouth amused.

'No—yes—you tried to——'

'It was a mutual thing,' Jake cut in. 'I can't deny

that I want you.' His grey eyes held hers and she felt as though she was drowning. With a great effort of will, she dragged her eyes away from his.

'Please let me past,' she said woodenly. 'We'll be late for dinner.'

Swearing under his breath, Jake took her chin between his fingers, searching her pale face, seeing her defeat, her intense weariness.

'You'll have to face it sometime,' he said harshly. She shrugged, not answering, and his hands dropped, allowing her to walk away.

She wore red silk for dinner, matching the dress with red shoes and the necklace Jake had given her. The food was delicious, served by the staff with silent efficiency, brought to the table from the silver chafing dishes that stood on a carved sideboard. The starter was *Esparragos trios dos salsas*, then stuffed crab or veal with vegetables and salad. For the sake of her hosts, Deborah tried to do justice to the meal, but she hardly tasted a mouthful. She was able to refuse the dessert—*flan al caramelo*—with the excuse that she was already replete, and settled for coffee, thick and black and bitter.

The conversation buzzed around her. Jake and Fernando had a lot of news to catch up on, and against her will, she found herself watching Jake. He was cool and witty and charming. She watched him smiling, at something Concepción said, and her heart lurched. In the candlelight, he looked dark and powerful and devastatingly attractive. She couldn't stop looking at him, her love shining in her face.

He moved his head, and their eyes met. His were suddenly very dark and very serious. He raised his glass to her in mock salute, and she felt herself flushing hotly. Silent communication flashed between

them, and she looked away, denying it, asking
Concepción something irrelevant about the ingredients
of the dessert.

The party broke up early. Concepción and Fernando
were leaving before dawn the following morning and,
as Concepción explained, she still had to supervise the
packing of their bags.

Deborah was tired. Pregnancy exhausted her, she
realised, as she allowed Jake to lead her down the long
dim corridors to their room. He walked beside her in
silence, not touching her, but she was aware of him
with every nerve in her body and by the time they
reached the bedroom, her heart was pounding like a
drum.

She stood aside, trembling, as he opened the door,
then preceded him into the room.

The lamps were lit, throwing pools of light into the
darkness. The bed had been re-made in their absence,
the velvet cover turned down. Deborah turned to Jake,
and found him watching her with dark blank eyes.

'I'm tired,' she said, her voice sharp.

'Go to bed,' he suggested with a faint smile.

'I can't——' Her eyes flashed anger at him,
frustration.

'Don't be ridiculous! He moved across the room,
looking out of the window.

Deborah stared at the broad tense sweep of his back,
tears filling her eyes. Why was he so cruel, so cold?
Her mouth trembled with self-pity.

'You'll have to sleep on the floor,' she told him
fiercely, as long seconds ticked by in strained silence.

'No.' He turned, his face hard. 'That bed is big
enough for both of us.'

'But . . .' she faltered, her eyes wide.

'Dammit, I'm not going to rape you,' he muttered

angrily. He moved towards her and she backed away, shaking. How could she possibly explain to him that she couldn't share his bed because she was more frightened of herself than of him?

'I didn't mean . . .'

'No? You're as transparent as glass.' His anger frightened her.

'Jake, look, I . . .' She didn't know what to say to him. Even now as he came towards her, tall and powerful in the dim light, she felt weak with longing for him. If they shared the same bed, would she have the self-control to stop herself begging him to make love to her?

He took her shoulders between his hands, hurting her. He watched her flinching with blank eyes.

'Very well. As you make your abhorrence to my touch so eloquently clear,' he drawled coldly, 'you have my promise that I won't lay a finger on you.' He let her go abruptly. 'Satisfied?'

Piqued and ridiculously frustrated, Deborah didn't answer. She walked into the bathroom and locked the door. She washed, then cleaned her teeth, staring at her reflection in the long mosaic-edged mirrors. Her cheeks were flushed, her eyes sparkling.

Jake was right, of course. The bed was enormous. Fear had made her unreasonable.

She brushed her hair slowly, putting off the moment when she would have to go back into the bedroom.

As she walked in, Jake was staring out of the window again. She said nothing, but climbed into the huge bed, head bowed. Sensing her presence he looked round. 'Decided to make the best of it?' he queried mockingly.

'I have no choice,' she flashed back.

'Of course you have,' he smiled, his eyes gleaming. Confused, Deborah turned on her side, pulling up the covers around her throat. She heard him laughing and gritted her teeth. She felt cold and very tense. Her tiredness had evaporated, leaving her wide awake and nervous. And it was ten nerve-racking minutes before she felt the mattress give and Jake slide in beside her. She lay perfectly still, her body rigid. Crazy that she should be this nervous, she thought, drawing a long shuddering breath.

Jake shifted beside her. 'Relax,' he murmured quietly. 'You're quite safe with me. I told you that I won't touch you, and I meant it.'

She listened to his voice, the low gentle timbre of it, and felt lonely.

'I'm cold,' she whispered into the darkness, not caring what she was inviting.

Jake sighed, moving, pulling the covers up over her bare shoulders. She rolled on to her back. 'Won't you hold me?' she begged softly.

She heard him swearing under his breath. 'You don't know what you're asking.'

She did know. She was being unfair, immediately regretting the impulse. 'I'm sorry.' She turned back on to her side, her mouth trembling, and he reached for her, as though he could not help himself, drawing her into his strong arms. She felt the smooth warmth of his body against hers, the heavy muscles of the arms that held her, and felt safe. She rested her head against his shoulder.

'For God's sake, keep still and go to sleep,' he said roughly.

She smiled, her loneliness gone, her eyelids drooping as she fell asleep. Against her breasts, Jake's heart beat its heavy rhythm. He held her tightly, his hands possessive, but when she woke next morning, she was alone.

CHAPTER TEN

DEBORAH woke early again, as she had done every morning lately. She lay back against the soft mound of pillows, desolation washing over her as she thought of Jake. Another day to face.

She climbed out of bed and strolled over to the window, flinging open the wooden shutters to let the sunshine in. The sky was pure blue, the air warm and scented with flowers, but the thought of facing her husband made her dawdle as she showered.

They had been in Seville for seven days now. The week had passed quickly and although she had liked Concepción and Fernando immediately, she was glad that she and Jake had the house to themselves. It meant that there was no need for exhausting pretence.

The situation hadn't improved. Jake slept in another bedroom, and Deborah lay alone every night, restless with longing for him, unable to pluck up the courage to go to him and admit her love. Her pride was long abandoned but some tiny part of her still held back. She still didn't trust him, certain he was lying about Leila. And because she didn't trust him, she couldn't give herself freely.

Memories of that time after their parting, memories of the pain that had seemed to last forever, contained her. She kept herself locked away. Even if she'd had the strength to admit her love, hadn't Jake made it very clear that his interest lay only in the child she was carrying?

There was still a fierce sexual tension between them,

but she knew that it wasn't enough. He didn't love her, and that would never change.

When she came downstairs, Jake was already there, scanning a Spanish newspaper, a cup of coffee in front of him. He looked up at her as she entered the room, his face revealing nothing of his thoughts. She felt herself trembling as their eyes met, but managed to greet him coolly.

'Did you sleep well?' he asked, with smooth mockery.

'Yes, thank you,' she lied, reaching for the coffee pot and finding it cold.

As she spoke Ana appeared, as though by silent command, carrying coffee, orange juice and a basket containing sweet rolls and *churros*.

In the silence that followed her departure, Deborah sipped orange juice, unable to touch any food, the warm smell of the fresh bread making her feel sick.

Jake glanced at her, his brows drawn together, frowningly. 'You should eat something,' he said, putting down the newspaper. 'Ana could bring you bacon or an omelette, anything you want.'

'I'm not hungry,' she replied, her stomach protesting at the food he mentioned.

'You should think of the child you're carrying.' His voice was very cool.

'I'm forced to think of it all the time,' she snapped, green eyes flashing fire. 'I'm sick nearly every morning.'

'Have you seen a doctor?'

'Yes, I have, which is why I don't need your advice on whether or not I should eat breakfast.' His eyes warned her to stop, but her lonely depression spurred her on. 'You're not the one who'll get as big as a house, you're not the one who'll suffer the pain, so don't tell me what I should be doing.'

His mouth hardened. 'Is that how you really see it?' he asked evenly.

'Is there another way?'

He was silent, but she could feel the probe of his eyes, as she poured herself a cup of coffee.

She knew she looked pale and tired, the dark circles round her eyes testimony to her sleepless nights. Would he attribute it to her pregnancy? She hoped he would, even though nothing could be further from the truth. The tension between them was getting to her. It was like walking a tight-rope.

They acted like polite strangers when they were together, never touching, never coming too close. Jake was kind to her, but he was also cool and withdrawn, a remote stranger with whom she had been thrown together in this beautiful house.

It couldn't go on, the waiting, the tension, it was like poison eating away at them both. She looked at him covertly and suddenly knew that it was affecting him too. There was a gaunt hollowed look about his face, the grey eyes burning like fire. And there was a tension in the way he moved, not noticeable to the casual observer, but noticeable to Deborah, who had watched him with the curious hunger of love. There was tension in his shoulders, in his hands, in the way he held his head, despite the cat-like grace of movement that remained unchanged.

She didn't know how long they could continue with this cruel charade, but sooner or later there would be an explosion. And while she waited for it, in the uneasy calm before the storm, her nerves were stretched as tight as wires.

Ana brought the mail as they sat together in strained silence. Jake had arranged to have all mail forwarded from England, while he researched his play.

'Anything for me?' Deborah asked lightly, not expecting anything.

Jake shook his head as he flicked through the envelopes. He picked up one, ripping it open impatiently, scanning the contents, his face totally expressionless, before slipping it into the pocket of his shirt. He said nothing, and Deborah noticed that the stamp was foreign. A woman, perhaps? The thought made her stomach clench with jealousy.

Jake put down the rest of the mail without opening any of it. 'Let's go sightseeing,' he suggested, watching her.

Surprised by the invitation, Deborah was silent for a moment. He spent most of his time shut away in the study working. It was an attractive proposition, more attractive than she cared to admit. 'Yes, I'd like to,' she smiled, her eyes meeting his briefly before veering away again.

They spent the day wandering around the old city, starting at the Giralda tower. Once inside the minaret, they walked up the ramps, looking out of the windows as they climbed higher. The wind whistled through the brick trellis-work, whipping Deborah's hair around her face. It was tiring, but much easier than walking up steps, and the view from the belfry was well worth the effort. Below them stretched the city. The Plaza de España, the bull ring, Triana, Los Remedios. Jake pointed them out, showing her the landmarks, his arm around her shoulders.

The red tiled roofs stretched into the distance, baking beneath the blinding Spanish sun. The patio of the Oranges, with its perfect symmetry, was a splash of cool green below. The iron bells above their heads chimed the hour, a deafening noise. Deborah laughed, exhilarated, surprised when Jake's dark head swooped, his mouth taking hers in a brief hard kiss.

Dizzily, she reached for his shoulders to steady herself, but he was already moving away, and she stared at the huge wooden framed clock, her eyes filling with tears.

Next to the Giralda, stood the cathedral—one of the largest Gothic churches in the world. Deborah wandered alone in the cold silence, deliberately keeping her distance from Jake. She was awed by the sheer size of the place, by the riches displayed in the antechambers off the main aisle. Everything seemed old and rich and faded, telling of a bygone age that could now only be guessed at by the parties of tourists clattering through with their guides. Many languages filled the hushed gloom, and the flashing of cameras, though not encouraged, sparkled in distant corners. Deborah felt alone, because of the vast space around her. The place was alive with the history of centuries, and she could understand why Jake found it so fascinating.

He found her half an hour later, gazing up at the enormous altarpiece.

'Let us build a church in such a way that those who see it will think we are crazy,' he quoted, smiling at her.

'Who said that?' she asked, returning his smile shyly.

'One of the members of the cathedral council in the fifteenth century,' he replied, taking her arm. 'Have you seen the monument to Christopher Columbus?'

Deborah shook her head, and allowed him to lead her to the huge coffin, held aloft by four larger-than-life allegorical figures. 'It's beautiful,' she whispered, walking round it, touching it with her fingers.

Jake watched her face. He had known she would like it.

They ate lunch under the orange trees of a streetside café. The slender, dark eyed waiter brought wine and a tray of tapas, which Deborah devoured, finding her appetite on tasting the flavours of ham and cheese and fish.

And in the late afternoon, they walked in the gardens of the Alcazar, past vaulted baths and lush palm trees and terracotta pots of geraniums that edged tiled fountains. It was a magical place that seemed to stretch on for ever, blocking out the city in the fading light. She was acutely aware of Jake walking beside her, and her heart ached. She wished she could share her delight in these magnificent gardens without restraint.

As they strolled down a narrow path lined with lemon trees, Jake turned to her. 'Tell me about Robert Stevens,' he said expressionlessly.

She wondered why he asked, but didn't dare to voice the question. It seemed right to tell him the truth here, as the dying sun streaked the sky with orange, in the peace and the greenery.

So she told him everything. That she and Robert had been childhood friends, that Frances had looked after both Oliver and herself after the death of their parents. She explained that she had never suspected Robert's true feelings for her, utterly surprised when he sought her out in America and proposed.

And she told him about the plane crash, the pretence, and Frances's gentle but unyielding persuasion. She told him everything, leaving nothing out. Not in anger this time, nor because she wanted revenge, but because it was important that he knew the truth.

Jake listened in silence, his face an expressionless mask, his body tense. When she had finished, he turned, taking her shoulders lightly in his hands. 'I'm sorry.'

Deborah shrugged, embarrassed. 'It doesn't matter. I know how it must have looked——'

'Yes.' He was abrupt. 'And since then, has there been anybody else?' The harshness of his voice brought colour to her face, and her heart was beating quickly.

'Why do you ask?' she prevaricated, knowing that if she told him she might be giving away everything.

'Because, dammit, I have to know.' His eyes held hers, pinning her mercilessly. She took a deep breath, unable to bear the torment she saw in his face. 'There's been nobody else,' she said quietly. 'Nobody.'

She heard the swift uneven intake of his breath without looking at him. She felt vulnerable, totally exposed. There were no secrets left, and she waited, head bowed, wondering what his reaction would be.

He swore violently, his mouth twisting with anger. 'Three years,' he said harshly. 'Three bloody years!'

Shaken, Deborah stared across the gardens. 'I don't know what you mean.' She touched her dry lips with the tip of her tongue. 'And I don't know why you brought me here. I want to go back to London.'

'No,' he said, one of his hands moving into her loose golden hair, winding the silken strands around his fingers.

'Why?' she whispered, staring up into his eyes. 'Why should you want to keep me here?'

'Because you belong to me. I'll never let you go again.' His face was hard, dark with emotion.

'I'll divorce you when the baby is born,' she told him bitterly.

'We'll see.' He was as cold as ice and she knew that he was still very angry. She felt like a child with threats that were not taken seriously.

'You let me go easily enough before,' she said, her cheeks burning.

'Because I believed you were sleeping with Robert Stevens.' His voice held a hard possessive jealousy, so deep that it frightened her. 'I wanted to kill him, and you. I searched high and low for you, but your stepbrother was always blocking my way. Perhaps he saw that I might well have done you an injury if I got to you. I realised that myself, and I had to let you go.'

'You accuse me?' she said bitterly. 'I can't believe your arrogance. You were the one who was unfaithful—you slept with Leila.'

'Did I?' He was impassive.

'I saw you.' His coolness fanned her hurt feelings into anger.

'You saw Leila in my bed,' he said flatly. 'That changes nothing. I won't let you go.'

'You won't be able to stop me,' she retorted in panic, trying to convince herself more than him. 'I won't live with you after the baby is born. I can't.' She paused, swallowing the lump in her throat.

'Why not?' His fingers tightened in her hair.

'Because I don't trust you. There have been too many women in your life. I'd spend all my time wondering who you were with, or worse, I'd walk in one day and find you in bed with somebody else,' she said rawly.

'That wouldn't happen, I promise you that,' he said slowly, then smiled. 'And if you wanted to make sure, you'd never leave my bed when I was in it.'

'No . . .' She pulled away from him, shaking. 'I believed you before and I was a fool. You told me that you wanted me, that you'd always want me, that there would never be anybody else. I won't believe you again.'

Jake watched her carefully, his eyes narrowing. 'I didn't lie to you,' he said expressionlessly. Then glancing at the gold watch on his wrist, 'It's time we were getting back.'

She rang Oliver that night while Jake was working. She felt a longing for a familiar voice, the beauty of her surroundings suddenly leaving her cold.

He snatched up the receiver almost immediately, and she suspected that he had been expecting Beatrice.

'Sorry if I'm a disappointment,' she said lightly. 'How are you?'

'Fine.' His voice was as purposely light as her own. They were both lying. 'Why on earth are you ringing me?' he asked. 'You're on your honeymoon. A postcard would have done, and I wasn't expecting that.'

'Honeymoon?' Deborah echoed cynically. 'Is that what this is?' She felt like laughing or crying. She wasn't sure which.

'Are you all right?'

Oliver's concern brought her back to her senses. 'I am. What about you?' She changed the subject quickly, avoiding further questions. 'Have you seen Beatrice?'

There was silence at the other end of the line, then Oliver said quietly. 'Yes, I've seen her.'

'And?'

'And nothing. It's over. They're moving to Bermuda. David has taken over an American banking company and they're moving for tax reasons.' He sounded very bitter, his voice scathing.

'I'm sorry.' It was inadequate. She could imagine how he must be feeling. He had given a lot away when he picked up the 'phone.

'No sympathy for God's sake,' he laughed humourlessly.

'But Oliver——'

'The incredible thing is that I'm relieved,' he cut in flatly. 'It hurts, it hurts like hell, but underneath I'm relieved, can you believe it? I burnt all her photographs, I really enjoyed doing it too. God, she had me for a fool!'

Deborah knew she should say something encouraging. She should say something reassuring about him finding somebody else, but she knew he wouldn't want to hear that. It wouldn't help. 'Oliver——'

'It's okay, I'll get over it, and at least I'll be able to get on with some work.' She felt him smiling. 'Don't worry about me. Tess has been holding my hand.'

'I wasn't,' she promised, because she heard the strength beneath his angry misery. He *would* get over it. Beatrice had always kept him on a string. He would never have been able to break it off. Now that she was moving away, she was the one who had decided to end the relationship. Oliver was free, because he couldn't change the situation. She felt sorry for him, but truthfully, she was glad. She had never really liked Beatrice, or what she was doing to Oliver. Then she realised what he had said. 'Tess?' she repeated with a smile.

'You heard me. But I'm not saying anything else, so get off the 'phone, get back to your husband and enjoy yourself. I don't want to hear from you again until you get back to London, okay? Unless of course, it's an emergency.'

She replaced the receiver with a sad smile. She hadn't been able to tell him about Jake and herself, something had held her back. Anyway, Oliver had his own problems, she thought, as she wandered slowly up the stairs to her empty room.

The following day Jake drove her out to the coast, to the Spanish resort of Playa Matascalanas. It was a modern resort, very popular with Sevillians, and it boasted miles of empty sandy beaches that stretched almost all the way to Huelva. They spent the day on the sands, swimming in the warm waters of the Gulf of Cadiz. Deborah felt self-conscious in her stylish one piece bathing costume. Her stomach hadn't started to swell yet, but her waistline was thickening slightly and she felt embarrassed beneath Jake's cool searching scrutiny.

'I'm ugly,' she said sharply, disconcerted by his silence. 'And soon, I'll hardly be able to move.'

He smiled with understanding. 'You're beautiful,' he said softly. 'So beautiful. Pregnancy suits you. Your eyes are sparkling, your skin is glowing with health and your body is perfect. You look radiant.'

'I'll bet,' she retorted, turning away, but inside, she was bursting with happiness at such compliments.

The sea was clear, the beach deserted beneath the hot sun. In the sand at the water's edge lay a huge ruined tower, tilting crazily, the ancient bricks covered with green moss. It looked dangerous, but it was so heavy it was safe. Deborah walked round it, her feet splashing coolly in the water. She looked at Jake and her mouth went dry. Wearing only brief black swimming trunks, his hard muscular body gleamed in the harsh light, the muscles rippling beneath tanned skin as he moved. She stared at his deep powerful chest and wanted him so, fiercely that it took her breath away. She dragged her eyes away, her body aching with unsatisfied need, and waded into the water to swim.

It was all so hopeless. She could see no end to it. They fought again and again, but nothing changed. He didn't love her and she would be trapped by that unbearable, unchangeable knowledge for the rest of her life.

They ate lunch under the rainbow parasols of a small café on the edge of the beach. The waiter brought *bocadillos* stuffed with cheese and sea-food, together with chilled white wine. Deborah picked at the food, her appetite non-existent. Jake watched her with narrowed eyes, his dark glance caressing when it rested on the slender grace of her body. When their eyes met, awareness shot between them, building as the meal continued, until it was unbearable. Deborah escaped back to the beach as soon as she could, thankful to reach for the protection of her sunglasses, ignoring the mockery she saw in his face. She lay sunbathing, her body relaxed, enjoying the warmth against her skin, and she watched Jake undetected, as he swam out into the sea. He was a powerful swimmer, his body cutting swiftly and cleanly through the water. When he returned, she stared at him. His body was graceful, dripping with water, the heavy muscles of his arms tensing, as he pushed his hair back from his face. He sat down beside her, and she drew a long shaking breath. She turned her head away in silence, relaxation gone, her body rigid.

'What are you frightened of?' he asked, as he lit a cigarette.

She looked at him from behind the smoked screen

of the glasses. 'I'm not frightened of anything,' she said airily.

He reached out and gently took the glasses from her nose. 'Tell me again,' he said softly, reading the confusion in her wide green eyes.

'Stop bullying me,' she replied huskily.

Jake sighed. 'Dammit, Deborah, I can't go on like this—it's driving me insane.' His voice became lower, softer. 'You're driving me insane.'

'The situation is of your own making,' Deborah retorted shakily. 'I didn't want this.'

'You want me,' he said roughly. 'Granted, not as much as I want you, but you do want me.'

'No.' She sat up, shaking like a leaf. 'You're wrong.'

'I guess the scars are too deep to forget,' Jake said flatly. 'But surely not too deep to heal. I know we've hurt each other——'

'I did nothing. It was you——' Her eyes flashed with pain and anger.

'You deliberately let me believe that you were seeing Stevens,' Jake bit out, cutting her off mid sentence.

Deborah lowered her head, flushing. She couldn't deny that. She felt cold, even though the sun was so hot. 'Can we go back to the house now? I'm tired.' There was pleading mingled with the defiance in her voice.

Jake's eyes probed her closed face. 'Sure, if that's what you want.'

'It is.' She stood up and pulled on her clothes.

They drove back through the baked arid countryside to Seville in silence. When they reached the house, Jake left her without a word, striding away across the courtyard. Deborah watched him go, her vision blurred with tears.

Ana met her at the door, her brown face creased with worry.

'A visitor,' she said with difficulty, her English not very good.

'Who is it?' She couldn't think of anyone who would visit them here. 'It is someone for *Señor* de Loza?' she asked, realising that this could be the only answer.

'No, *señora*, to see you and *Señor* Logan. She has been here many hours.' Ana was obviously agitated which seemed to add to the mystery.

Deborah followed the maid into the house, only to find herself face to face to Leila, as she entered the lounge. She could hardly believe her eyes.

The other girl looked pale and beautiful, her light linen suit immaculate, which made Deborah very aware of her salt-stained shorts and T-shirt.

For a moment she was too stunned to speak, but Leila's malicious smile brought her to her senses.

'What are you doing here?' she asked quietly.

'Where's Jake?' Leila demanded wildly, not answering. 'Where is he? I want to see him. I've been waiting for hours and I haven't been able to get a word of sense out of that stupid maid.'

'I don't know where Jake is,' Deborah said honestly. 'Why have you come here?' She knew she should offer Leila hospitality, but the febrile glitter in the other girl's eyes frightened her, and she found herself wondering if Leila was ill.

'Won't you sit down?' she suggested as calmly as she could. 'And I'll ask Ana to find Jake.'

'That maid is on your side. You're trying to keep him away from me, that's why you've come here,' Leila said, and smiled, a crazy terrifying smile. 'Tess told me yesterday that you're pregnant.'

Deborah frowned. Oliver, she thought.

'Well, it won't work, you won't keep him. He's mine. He loves me.' She took a step forward and Deborah backed, really afraid now. There was something dangerous about Leila, something in her eyes, something in the way she was talking, something vicious and frightening.

'Leila, please sit down,' she said again, thinking, where are you, Jake? This is your problem, not mine, and I don't think I can cope.

Leila's smile faded. 'I can do anything,' she said, her voice strangely quiet. 'Jake brought me from France to live with him. You see he loves me, not you. I'll tell him that it's not his baby you're carrying. I kept you away from him for three years. I enjoyed seeing your face when you found me in his bedroom. Jake was angry, you poisoned his mind.' She rambled on as though talking to herself.

Realisation dawned on Deborah in a sudden blinding flash. She had been wrong. *For three years she had been wrong.* 'You did it deliberately, didn't you?' she said, smiling herself now, a little hysterical. She remembered what Leila had said at the wedding. 'I did it once and I'll do it again.'

'Oh yes,' Leila said coolly, pleased with herself and anxious to reveal all the details. 'I was looking out of the window and I saw your car. I went to Jake's room to tell him, but he was in the shower, so I got into bed and waited.'

Deborah felt her legs trembling and sank into the nearest chair. Jake had been telling the truth all the time. She had refused to believe him.

'Jake threw me out when he found me, but you'd already gone,' Leila continued, smiling.

'How could you?' Deborah whispered, her heart pounding. 'How could you?'

Leila moved closer. 'I'm *glad* I did it. I *hate you*.'

She lifted her hand. She's going to hit me, Deborah thought in horror, unable to move a muscle.

'Leila!' Jake's voice was like a whiplash in the silence. He moved into the room.

'Deborah's done nothing. Why do you want to hurt her?'

'She's trying to take you away from me,' Leila said wildly, but her hand dropped, and Deborah let out her breath on a long shaking sigh of relief.

'No, she's my wife,' Jake said quietly. 'I want her.'

Deborah looked at him. He filled the room with his presence, his calm strength, and she felt safe.

'How can you want her?' Leila demanded emotionally. 'I love you!'

'But I don't love you.' His voice was gentle but firm.

Leila began crying noisily, then the room seemed full of people—Ana, and a small man with a leather case. A doctor, Deborah thought thankfully.

She stood up and walked out of the room, unnoticed. She walked into the courtyard, breathing deeply of the warm air. Her head was spinning with all that had happened, but one thought soared above the confusion. Jake had not lied to her. He and Leila had never been lovers. She sat down on the tiled edge of the fountain, and let her hand trail in the cold water. The day was losing its heat, night beginning to fall around her. Leila had caused so much heartbreak in their lives. Could the damage ever be repaired?

Jake found her deep in thought as he strolled outside half an hour later.

'I've been looking for you,' he said deeply.

She looked up into his dark familiar face and smiled. 'I've been here.'

'She didn't hurt you?'

'No, I'm just stunned.'

'She told you the truth?' His eyes were very dark, very serious.

'Yes. And I'm sorry I called you a liar. You should have told me.'

'I did. You didn't believe me.'

'No.' She smiled at him and his eyes narrowed on her face.

'I didn't even know what she'd done until you told me,' he said harshly. 'I remember finding her in my bed, I didn't know you'd even been to the house. The day after the wedding, I confronted her with what you'd told me and she admitted everything.'

Deborah was silent, ashamed of herself. 'Where is she now?'

He frowned. 'Dr Clemente has given her a sedative, and she's been taken to the local hospital. I've arranged for her to be flown back to England and transferred to a hospital there as soon as she's well enough to travel. Clemente is a good doctor—she'll be well looked after.'

'What's the matter with her?'

His shoulders lifted wearily. 'A complete breakdown. She's been ill for some time now, but nobody thought it would come to this.'

'But, why?' Deborah shook her head, puzzled.

'I don't know. She's had a very hard life. The main thing is that she'll get better.'

'She said she loved you,' Deborah said quietly.

Jake shook his head. 'She doesn't. It's part of her illness, an obsessional thing, I guess. That will go too, as she recovers.' He touched her hair with gentle fingers. 'You do believe that I never touched her, never wanted to?'

Deborah nodded, her face sombre. 'Yes. But——'

'But what?' His face was tense, his hand suddenly still against the softness of her hair.

'Why did you bring her from France to live in England?' It was a question she had wanted to ask for three years. Jake reached into his pocket and pulled out the letter he had been reading at breakfast the morning before. He handed it to her. 'I've been waiting for the right moment to show you this. Read it,' he said expressionlessly.

'I——'

'Read it.'

The envelope had a French stamp on it. She took the letter out. It was from a firm of solicitors in Paris, confirming after thorough investigation . . .

'She's your *sister*!' Deborah exclaimed, the letter dropping from her suddenly nerveless fingers.

'Half sister,' he corrected grimly. 'Another one of my mother's affairs.'

'How did you find out.'

'I didn't know for certain until yesterday—I was pretty sure, but I needed that final proof, so that I could make you believe me.' He ran a tired hand through the darkness of his hair. 'Some years ago, I found an old diary of my mother's, and from the details in that, I managed to trace Leila, through the French side of her family. She was living in poverty in Paris, earning a living any way she could. I had to help her. It seems that my mother had just abandoned her, left her with her lover, Leila's father. He's long dead, but he treated her pretty badly, which is why she ended up in Paris, fending for herself.'

'That's terrible,' Deborah breathed, able to feel sympathy for Leila now, sadness at the tragedy of her life. It was no wonder she had focused on Jake as her saviour, her protector. He must have seemed like some sort of God to her, rescuing her from what sounded like a hellish life.

She could also understand now why Jake had been so violently angry about Robert, why he had insisted that she married him. His child would always know its father and its mother. History would not repeat itself. Only one question remained unanswered. Where did she stand?

Jake took her hands and pulled her gently to her feet. 'I don't want to talk about Leila,' he said softly. 'I want to talk about you and me.'

Worry prickled down Deborah's spine. She felt unsure of herself, certain that he was going to ask her to leave.

'There's nothing to talk about,' she said quickly. 'I want to go back to London, alone.' She would go of her own free will, before he asked her to go.

Jake shook his head, his face hard. 'I meant what I said, I won't let you go.'

'No?' She smiled at him provocatively, seeing something in his eyes that made her heart stop beating.

'No.' He tilted her face in his hand, his eyes dark and sure and possessive. 'I love you,' he murmured raggedly. 'I loved you from the moment I first saw you.' He bent his head, kissing her mouth hungrily. 'You rose from that stream as the light faded and your untouched beauty took my breath away. I knew then that you were the one I'd been waiting for all my life, and I knew I'd never be able to let you go.' He kissed her again, and groaned. 'It left me half dead when we parted. I made everyone's life a bloody misery.'

Deborah laughed. 'I know, Tess told me.'

He smiled, smoothing her hair back from her

temples. 'I suspected she was up to something. I seem to have been fighting for you every day of my life. I thought if we came here, I'd have you to myself.' He drew breath harshly. 'Tell me you love me, Deborah.'

'I told you,' she whispered, trembling, her heart soaring with happiness. He loved her, he had always loved her.

'In the heat of passion, yes, and you hated admitting it.'

'I hated myself,' she corrected gently. 'Because I wanted you so much, despite—well, despite everything.' She touched his wide shoulders, and felt the muscles clenching beneath her hands.

'Tell me,' he said again.

She reached up, and kissed his strong sensual mouth. 'I love you, Jake,' she whispered into his throat. 'I loved you right from the start, even though I was too young and too foolish, and I never ever stopped. I'll always love you——'

The words stopped as he took her mouth, his arms tight, holding her against the hard strength of his body until she was dizzy with need for him.

When he lifted his head, she swayed against him, her body aching.

'How do you feel about the baby?' he murmured, kissing her face.

'Oh, I'm glad, so glad,' she admitted, smiling. 'Even when I first found out, I wanted it, because it was a part of you. Oh, Jake, I've been so jealous, of Leila, of Caroline Winters, of everybody you smiled at.'

His powerful arms tightened around her. 'It's always been you, my love,' he said deeply. 'There hasn't been a single second when I haven't thought of you. I tried to forget you, and I did see other women, but it was pointless. I didn't want them, I wanted

you—so much, I thought I was going mad sometimes.'
He smiled wryly. 'I didn't mean to rush things when
we met again, but I couldn't help myself. I bought the
flat for Tess and Leila, so that the house would be
ours. I had it all planned out. I was crazy with jealousy
about Robert Stevens and I couldn't chance losing you
again. When I found out from Oliver that you were
pregnant, I grabbed my chance with both hands.'

Deborah laughed. 'How unscrupulous. I thought
you were only interested in the baby.'

'It was you,' he admitted huskily. 'God, how I love
you.'

Deborah kissed his tanned throat. There was so
much to say, so much to catch up on from three
wasted years, but right now, she didn't want to talk,
and when she looked into the burning depths of his
eyes, she knew that he didn't either.

'I want you,' she murmured provocatively. 'Please
take me to bed.'

Without a word, he lifted her into his strong arms
and carried her inside, upstairs to his bed. He
undressed her, reining his deep impatience, his hands
sure and gentle, his grey eyes holding hers in the dim
light.

'You're so beautiful,' he murmured, bending his
dark head to kiss her breasts.

'So are you.' She moaned as he touched her,
knowing that she could give now, without reserve,
everything she had been holding back. 'Ah, Jake, I
love you.'

'Show me,' he said with quiet command.

She laughed, happiness filling her, setting her free.

'I will,' she promised tenderly, and secure in his
love, she began to kiss his mouth.

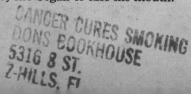

Harlequin Presents

Coming Next Month

Available in September wherever paperback books are sold, or through Harlequin Reader Service:

In the U.S.
P.O. Box 1397
Buffalo, N.Y.
14240-1397

In Canada
P.O. Box 2800, Postal Station A
5170 Yonge Street
Willowdale, Ontario M2N 6J3

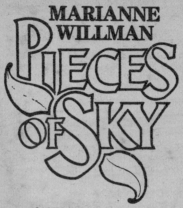

A terrible family secret drives Kristi Johannssen to
California, where she finds glamor, romance
and...a threat to her life!

BEYOND THE RAINBOW

MARGARET CHITTENDEN

Power and elegance, jealousy and deceit, even murder, stoke
fires of passion in this glittering novel set in the fashion world
of Hollywood, on the dazzling coast of Southern California.

ATTRACTIVE, SPACE SAVING BOOK RACK

Display your most prized novels on this handsome and sturdy book rack. The hand-rubbed walnut finish will blend into your library decor with quiet elegance, providing a practical organizer for your favorite hard-or soft-covered books.

Only $9.95

Approximately 16" x 8" when assembled

Assembles in seconds!

To order, rush your name, address and zip code, along with a check or money order for $10.70 ($9.95 plus 75¢ postage and handling) (New York residents add appropriate sales tax), payable to *Harlequin Reader Service* to:

In the U.S.

Harlequin Reader Service
Book Rack Offer
901 Fuhrmann Blvd.
P.O. Box 1325
Buffalo, NY 14269-1325

Offer not available in Canada.

BKR-1

HIST-A-1